Chapter 1 - The Pub

"Today's H-Harry's a-anniversary, I h-hate him," Cal said to Denise while looking into his beer."

Denise and Cal shared a quiet conversation at the end of the long table.

Denise said, "They didn't call it Achlys for nothing, mate, goddess of misery and darkness. Ain't that the truth, but it's a long time back, Cal. Let it go. You'd just have died with him, and who would have led the attack on the ridge? Who would have charged into Travertine?"

Denise took a long pull from her mug then added, "Harry ended the war single handedly. Let him be the legend, Cal. You take care of Sybil and Trevor for him. That's your job."

Petey shouted from the far end of the long table, "Cal, you should come! If you come, everyone will come."

Cal looked away, hiding the sudden moisture problem on his face. The airlock engaged from outside and dust blew in another grime covered outlander slapping a cloud off his pants and duster. The newcomer greeted the long table, "What a surprise to find you all here ... again, and again." Then he nodded, "Cal, Denise."

Looking down, Cal said, "Cooksey."

Tony Cooksey continued greeting old faces further into the pub.

"Hi Cooksey," Petey said, "Come have a seat after you get yourself sorted out." Turning to Cal, Petey said, "Alastair says there'll be dancers there."

Cal said, "Doesn't sound like f-fun, Petey. Any chance one of the d-d-dancers is a women with red h-hair?"

"As a matter of fact one is! There you go, Cal. Red heads love big fellas. She's just waiting for a big man like you!"

Cal started to say and finally got the words out, "If there's a b-blonde with a mole on her ch-ch-cheek those are probably the

W-Welker sisters. They're pretty well traveled. And keep a hand on your money. It seems to go m-m-m-missing when they're about. Besides Petey," Cal redirected the conversation, "A-Angela and Denise here are women. I'll bet they could manage a b-boogaloo or two."

"In your dreams, Cal," Denise said.

Cal shot back, "F-Funny you should s-say, why just last n-n-night ..."

Denise smiled while placing her sidearm on the table in front of her. The group erupted with laughter.

Petey turned to another mate at the table, "Avinash, when was the last time you danced with a woman, in person I mean, up close?"

"Ah, that was five years ago at Wellington space port. This one came right up to me and took my hand."

Petey continued, "See what I mean! We should all go!" Petey said, and then addressed Cooksey walking over, brew in hand, "There's a party at The Wallow. Dancers will be there."

Big Skippy Walker also approached the table mocking, "C-C-Cal you should g-g-go. You might find your m-m-mum ..."

Cal, easily the largest man most had ever seen, spun out of his seat in a blur and shot a hand to Skippy's throat cutting off his words along with air and blood flow. Cal's trailing hand stopped Skippy's reach for his pistol. Cal slammed the thinner man against the stone wall while Skippy vainly grabbed at Cal's massive wrist. Cal's dark face got darker red with rising veins inches from his opponent. Denise stepped to Cal's side.

Skippy's crew at the back table stood drawing hardware, but stopped when they heard weapons charging around them, from Chico and Wing Lu at the back table, Angela behind the bar, and everyone at the long table. When they faced forward even Denise had her interrupter aimed at them.

Chico said, "Think hard, mates. Those are the First Brigade Honey Badgers, fearless, vicious. Not one of them is afraid of nothing."

Ruin of Time

K N Boyle

Other works by K N Boyle

The Random Killing
Flood Tide

Their decision still in doubt Chico lifted his pistol higher and added, "Collin, don't make me put a whole in that nice vest you won off me. You'll be the first one gone."

Denise said to the big man struggling in Cal's grasp, "Cal's pretty quick, isn't he Skippy, but you're not, are you? Regular drongo. This is just like last time you said something blindingly moronic."

Skippy may not have heard Denise as his eyes rolled back. Cal let him drop in a pile.

Denise said over her shoulder, "No worries mob, your mate's just sleeping off a stupidity bender." Then she patted Cal's shoulder and coaxed, "You drubbed him good, Cal. Now let's move along and see about that brew of yours, right? Cal?"

Cal, still fuming at the heap on the floor, finally said, "Don't want to hurt him too bad. Might need target practice later. He shouldn't talk about my mum."

Denise led him back to the table saying, "Well, didn't he cure your stutter for a minute?"

"But I don't stutter in combat ... or bar f-fights. Oh, right."

The room took a deep breath to relieve tension, and Petey repeated his request while the mob drug Skippy to the airlock, "So what about dancers, who's in with me? Tony, you in?"

Tony Cooksey pulled out a chair for himself , "Cal, there's a package at the post for a Dearman. Isn't he the farmer up the ridge from your place?"

"Yeah, that's him. I'll p-pick it up on my w-way out."

"Then you best get moving, mate. Second moon's up and there's a creeper rolling in."

"That's it for me g-gents, ladies." Cal lifted his mug and proclaimed, "Harry Bolger." All at the table lifted mugs and answered, "To Harry."

Cal said, "I'm for it n-now."

As Cal engaged the airlock he heard Tony say, "No Petey, I'm not giving you a lift to Wellington!"

Chapter 2 – Home Front

Cal strapped his shipment onto the sled and tucked Dearman's single pouch into the lock box in the cab of his dune skimmer, checking over his shoulder at the slow moving wall of airborne dirt rolling towards Settlers Grove outpost. The mag coils fired and the skimmer moved. Cal thought about his mum, wondered where she was. He revisited every memory of his father up to the day he was gunned down in front of their shack. Driving through the tragic memories of parent's love and misery, Cal would get home in time to seal the doors and activate the capacitor array to collect static electricity from the storm. Feeders checked and vapor injectors cleared of salt, Cal went to his desk to check on assignments for the next day.

Shipping agent for Red Sky conglomerate was a fancy name for virtual bouncer, electronic enforcer, and cajoler, what ever was required to get well paid people to do the job they were well paid for - namely taking the right cargo off freighters at the right port, and putting the right cargo on before flying away. Flying was the part everyone wanted to do. Correct loading and unloading were most of the problems. Occasionally he personally went to the space port if requested. No one argued with his large presence, massive hands, dead even stare, and the near god like authority Red Sky gave to shipping agents on remote planets.

"You'd think I'd get paid for travel time," he said to the darkening screen with a sigh. "Well, come on Sybil," Cal said to the long eared fox like creature, "Let's catch some sleep in the dark for a change."

Sybil shared Cal's home especially during storms. She had her own underground entrance courtesy of the previous owner whose meager remains were buried outside under three feet of hard pan. The plaque on the grave read:

Captain Harry Bolger

Born ?

Died 23.7.2526 on Onyx, Achlys system

Beloved leader, devoted friend

Sacrificed himself in life and in death

Cal would clear the sediment away after the storm. He always did.

Chapter 3 – Overtime

The buzzing woke him. The light from the monitor confirmed he was being hailed. Sybil scampered into the wooden crate hiding her entrance and down the tunnel.

"Cal Workman here."

"Caleb Workman," the dispatcher droned, "Problem with a delivery clearing port authority at Port Wellington. Ship is overdue for departure. You are required to see to it personally. Shipping documents uploaded to your remote."

Cal looked down at the handheld's status bar sliding across the screen. "Documents r-received, Workman clear."

Cal opened the door to a clear twilight sky. Cardea's sky never darkened. When the second sun further off approached setting, and just before the main star, Coleus rose, the sky dimmed giving some relief from the heat and light. Cal's skimmer made the zigzag trip up the ridge. As usual Lares Dearman met him outside the home.

"Hey Lares. I-I need to run to W-Wellington. Can one of the boys check on th-things for me?"

"Caleb, good storm last night. My batteries are charged for months. How did you fare down below?"

"N-No time to check, bit of a hurry. Oh, and I've a p-post for you. Small parts by the sound of it."

"Take care now, Caleb. Even with food shortages I can buy more pigs. Good neighbors are even scarcer. A lot of traffic up there just before the storm, some big ones too, and at least one Confederation bird. They've either cleared off or landed. Couldn't tell with the creeper coming."

"Good to know. I'll probably be seeing a f-few of them."

"Write down the numbers if you see 'em. And don't post 'em."

"I know Lares, I'll b-bring them by."

Following one rift valley then another to avoid cross winds Cal made the trip to the first check point outside Wellington in two hours, the best he could hope for. The storm cleared the air allowing the coils to better connect with the planet's mag fields. The port was south of the city past the second check point. Cal could see a Confederation logo on a sleek executive transport sitting on the pad. Traffic rarely got past Lares' observation.

Chapter 4 - The Pilot

A concussive sound followed the plume of dust rising from a pad outside Red Sky hangar. Cal shook his head hoping they would not try again before he arrived. He sped directly to the freighter flashing his Red Sky security badge at the guards who knew him by sight. Sliding the skimmer out of harms way he ran to the freighter and pounded on the hatch. After a minute the hatch pulled back showing an interrupter inches from his face.

"Put that thing down or I'll take it away from you.," Cal said grabbing the sides of the hatch and pulling himself into the ship, weapon following him.

"I want to know what moron is flying this ship!" Cal bellowed into the hold up toward the catwalk above, where the ship's bridge access stood open. A tall woman dressed in a jump suit stepped out, jumped to the first landing, leaned out hooking an arm around an unattached support and spiraled down to the bottom. Cal knew only experienced crewmen performed this feat.

The intense, striking face with piercing dark eyes sent Cal's brain in multiple directions. Recovering he said, "Are you the c-captain?"

A loose pony tail of jet black hair framed the eyes focusing on Cal said, "Yes, I am the moron. How do I get this ship skybourn?"

Cal fought to keep focus. He finally said, "Sh-Show me your cert n-n-number for the shipment and R-Red Sky ID."

Scanning the ID and certificate of lading Cal got a green light on his hand held. He said, "Your engine m-mounts are modified."

The woman did not look away.

Cal said, "N-Not the original engines. Y-Y-ou should know something about the ship you are f-f-flying. Cheap replacements come from l-l-landers or solar freighters."

"We just commandeered this ship. We've had pirates on our tail for the last three ports. They shot heat shields and stabilizers off our transport. If we don't get skybourn quickly they will find us and shoot off more personal parts."

Cal said, "Okay, n-now we're all f-friendly, here's the p-problem. Your port engine is a l-lander engine. St-St-Starboard, I can't tell what it is, but landers take off s-s-slowly. Goose the juice and you'll f-fall out of the sky. So ... take .. off ... s-s-slowly. You also need to s-spike your fuel to get the spray right. Anything with alcohol will work. In tight places you can even piss into the fuel port. Not recommended but it'll get you by. What do you have on board?"

The pilot said, "We have champagne. Jamie, get one of the cases."

Jamie put his interrupter away and pulled a wooden case from a large container. He pried the top off revealing 12 bottles of champagne cushioned in shredded paper..

Cal yelled up to crew men on the catwalk, "One of you f-fellas run and charge the igniters. Jamie you and ...," Cal looked at his hand held then said, "Jacquelin open three of these b-bottles. There's a s-spike tube built into most of the f-freighters super structure."

Jacquelin handed Cal a bottle while she started untwisting the wire frame on the cork. Cal followed her example. Three loud pops later Cal found a pipe with a screwed on plumbing cap. A sign stating, 'No Open Flames While Uncapped' was posted above it.

Cal poured the first two in, then took a big drink of the third and poured the rest in.

"Was that necessary?" Jacquelin asked.

Smiling Cal said, "A s-swig for good luck. N-Never seen a bottle of champagne before."

"I suppose you'll need paid for your service," Jacquelin said as someone pounded outside the lower hatch.

Cal said to Jamie, "Hold a minute there, Jamie." Then to Jacquelin he said, "A p-please and thank w-wouldn't kill you now."

In a maintenance locker Cal pulled a two-handled greasy power tool, put a long cartridge into the side slot, slapped a battery pack onto the back of it, and said, "All right, now we can have a civilized conversation. Jamie, open the hatch from the far side."

The lock disengaged and sizzling electron particle bolts blazed into the hold. Cal stepped close and fired the nail gun from the side hitting the shooters fore arm, tearing the shooter away from the door, impaling the gun arm onto the hard pan launch pad. With the shooter whipped aside and screaming, Cal stepped in front of the open hatch and spiked the next man in line high in the chest throwing him backwards, also pinning him to the pad.

Retreating boots gave Cal permission to jump down and fire at the two retreating men. Four more nails from Cal's nail gun caught one low bending him backward at a weird angle. The last jumped behind storage cases ahead of the twelve inch spikes piercing the container, but ricocheting off the metallic contents.

"Jamie, toss me more nail boxes!" When the boxes landed Cal shouted, "Fire up and lift off slowly!" Cal slammed another box home when he heard Jamie shout, "We're port locked!"

Cal pulled out the hand held and cleared the status, "You're good. Leave now!"

The roar began and built slowly with the usual accompanying sand storm kicked up by the engines' backwash. Cal dashed for protection, covering his eyes. He picked out the sound of small arms pinging off the fuselage, but he couldn't rise yet.

As the blast lessened Cal spoke into the hand held, "Barney, I've got a few armed bad guys in the Red Sky hangar! Could use your help!"

"Cal, I'm walking into the offices now. Confederation officers called me. Don't shoot anyone. They could be Confeds."

The standoff silence was broken by Barney's shout, "Cal, come on out. Confeds are pulling out just like Point Casino." Cal stood. It was good to have trusted friends.

"Here Cal, I'll take that." Barney said as Cal walked closer. Barney grunted under the weight of the tool Cal handed him. Barney continued, "Cal, a lieutenant stayed behind to ask you questions. I let 'em know you're the shipping agent and they backed off. They wanted you dead, I'm sure, or at least have you turned over, but no one wants to bother Red Sky. They settled for some talk. Hope you don't mind."

Entering the offices a lieutenant stood as Cal neared, "Please sit down, Sergeant Workman ."

Cal said, "Be thankful I'm not pressing charges. You attacked an authorized Red Sky freighter, and there's no sergeants about. Mister Workman is heading down to The Wallow for a beer. You want to talk, that's where I'll be," and he brushed past the lieutenant who fell in behind the limping Barney.

Chapter 5 - Repercussions

Several days later Cal made it back to Settlers Grove. Denise found him at the long table.

"You missed a few days, Cal. Get messed up in the troubles at Wellington?"

Cal continued looking into his beer.

Denise asked, "How many?"

"T-Two ... and a h-half."

Denise put her arm as far around Cal's shoulders as she could reach, "Cal, before any of the mob get here I need to tell you something." Cal did not look up. Denise continued, "Captain made you swear to take care of Sybil, Trevor, and the girls for him. Do you know why he asked you and not the rest of us? He knew the mercs would be drooling to get you. They would use you up, tear you up, and move on. He gave you the farm so you'd have a home and some that need you." She waved her arm around the pub, "and some mates that need you. This job of yours with big Red, don't let it own you."

Cal said, "You know those m-mercs who came round to collect me a few t-t-times?"

"Yeah."

"I s-saw one of 'em in Wellington."

"What'd he say?"

Cal took a swallow and said, "Ah, not m-much. He had a g-grounding s-spike in his chest."

Denise looked doubtful, "Naw, can't be. Confeds don't use mercs."

"M-Maybe he switched o-over."

"Mercs are in it for the money. The pay won't sway 'em. Maybe this was off the books," she said wanting to avoid the more difficult subject, Denise said, "Hey, while you were out the ruling coalition fell apart. There's new faces at the top now. Angela has the news on screen. Angela, a little volume."

Cal looked up at the screen above the bar. He stood up and said, "Who is that?"

"Pieter LeBura, new confed premier. Do you recognize him?"

"N-No, but the w-w-woman standing behind him was in W-Wellington. A-Angela, can you pause and tap the dark haired woman."

Angela said, "She's a real looker, Cal. A bit over your gun sights."

"M-M-More than you know."

The pop up screen read, Jacquelin Jammula - security detachment, Confederation Allied Party ..." The remainder of the information was weight, height, genetics ID, the usual personal data.

Cal said, "I don't believe it!"

"Me neither," Denise said, "She's gotta weigh more than 134 units. She's paid off the information ministry."

Angela laughed, "Or they weighed her on Onyx."

"No," Cal said, "she was the c-captain of the ship in Wellington."

Avinash and Tony came through the door lock. Angela blurted out before anyone said hello, "Cal killed a merc in Wellington!" Denise gave her a withering stare.

"How many days ago," Avinash asked.

Tony guessed, "That'd be about five days ago. You'd think they'd be all over your place long before today. Did you see 'em, Cal?"

Denise looked at Cal and said, "No, he was staying away to keep us out of the action. Pretty selfish there, mate. What's your plan?"

"I p-p-plan on going home and taking c-care of the farm."

Angela said, "And just let them come? Not bloody likely, Caleb. Time to gear up, team!"

"N-N-No, that is e-exactly what I d-d-don't want," Cal said, "I don't want to bury any more friends."

"Neither do we, Sergeant Workman," Denise said.

The door lock opened on a young boy with dirty tear tracks on his cheeks, "Mr. Workman, Andrew is trapped inside your house!"

"What happened, Chris?"

"Watched him from ridge," desperate sobs and gulps of air from the boy, and then he said, "Armed men came while he was inside. They were breaking things and there were blasts," Chris said crying. "Papa sent this."

A crumpled paper read: seven men inside, small arms, lots of ammo. Two phase cannons on high points, two men each, two birds circling high, one bird in orbit. Dearman gave coordinates for the phase cannons, and comm IDs for the birds.

Tony said, "Probably killed Trevor and the girls."

"They didn't get all of them," Cal added.

"I get the bird in orbit!" Avinash said.

"Okay," Denise said, standing, "I need fifteen minutes to get us all launched with gear. I'll take Angela for the circling birds. Tony, get Wing Lu and Chico. Sand suits and shields everyone. I'll get the locker open. Where's Petey?"

"He's sleeping one off," Tony said.

"Good, makes him more dangerous. Wake his skinny butt. We're going low comm 714. Everyone move and comm check. Cal, you're not sitting this out. Get your skimmer over to the hangar."

Denise added, "Chris, honey, I need to to go to William's house and stay there for now."

Cal knew it was pointless to argue. The old team was on autopilot moving as a machine. The last mission they had taken on was rescuing Wing Lu from a deal gone bad in the sand sea crater. They lost Miranda that day. It was what they trained for, dreamed of, breathed, talked about, waiting for the next adventure until it was their last. Training was the two edged sword. Warriors created and thrown into the latest trouble only to be discarded when the trouble was resolved with no training for re-entering society. This was the reason so many lived on planets like Cardea, a waste land polite society avoided.

Denise lived at the hangar with Angela running off-planet transport company D & A Excursions. Both were top combat pilots, many decorations, many kills.

"Where's your skimmer?" Angela asked when Cal walked in. "You're the bait on this bait and switch. Bring it through the people door in the back. Wing Lu, thanks for coming."

Angela barked, "Captain on deck!"as Denise walked out of their living quarters in her finest sand suit and took charge. "Cal, we need your skimmer. Comm check, P1."

Cal trotted to the back double door and guided the skimmer inside. The floor of the open space in the hangar was already lifting upward on one side revealing a large freight door. Angela disarmed security and opened the weapons store.

"Cal, you won't look armed."

"Comm check P3," all heard in their ear sets from Avinash, "P3 enroute."

"Comm up, P3. Understood," Angela responded.

Chapter 6 – Time to Think

Later Cal was back in the pub giving the team time to insert quietly. He pulled out his handheld and clicked Barney in Wellington. "Barney, how's the feet?"

"Same as always, Cal. They hurt. You coming back here soon? Let's get a brew."

"Soon mate. I'm looking for a shipment of off worlders. Would have come loaded down."

The pause on the comm spoke volumes. Then Barney said, "Haven't seen much, couple executive types, a few miners. Nothing scheduled soon. What are you looking for?"

"Big Red was thinking a shipment might get diverted here. Just checking."

"No mate. Dead as that Travertine ghost town."

"All right then. Talk to you soon, Barn."

"Barney clear."

Chapter 7 – Ready, Steady, Go!

Cal walked out the pub airlock and started moving the skimmer out of town. The reminder of the ghost town woke sleeping memories Cal tried hard to forget as he entered the narrow canyon knowing he was being watched from orbit high and low. The end of the canyon came in sight and Cal heard in his ear set, "PC north friendly." The first phase cannon was taken.

Thoughts ran through his mind how the mercs would come after him to protect their reputation, and get payback. It suddenly occurred to him the big effort they expended was because the mercs expected an armed response.

His eyes widened and he shouted, "P1, 2, and 3, pull back. It's a trap. PC north abandon. You're zeroed in. Pull back all forces!"

Avinash said, "S1, I totally got this ... Oh shit! Two more high orbits just appeared! I'm running. Hopefully they'll follow."

"P1 and 2 already engaged," Angela said. Cal heard the propulsion scream over head as multiple fighters shot across the atmosphere in high speed maneuvers. Denise added, "I count five, make that six marks. A lot of targets up here. Playing canyon chase. Duck your head."

"PC west is friendly but withdraw ..." A distant explosion, followed by multiple concussions thudded echoes off the rock walls. Then Denise roared past vertically, wings spread for maximum turn flexibility. One fighter chased the canyon, two more waited up top for her exit. Behind Cal's position a granite protrusion removed the top half of the craft trailing Denise. Fire, smoke, fuel, and a torrent of pieces parts rained down to the canyon floor behind him.

Cal shielded the skimmer before it left the concealment of the gorge making electronic scanning and targeting impossible. As he cleared the last rocks electron rifles guessed his position from the dust trail. On the rise up to his farm he powered up his personal shield, and rolled off. The skimmer continued forward while he took cover scanning the rises and the ridge for muzzle flashes.

The rocky knob of phase cannon north was no longer a knob. An outcropping for the west cannon was intact but the slope leading up to it was pock marked by fighter blasts.

"GS2 in place, P1 and 2, PC west friendly. Waltz your boyfriends by here please." Petey was alive!

Cal called, "You are still the luckiest bastard I've ever met!"

Angela called out, "One of 'em shot my butt. I don't like him any more."

"You bring 'em by. I'll show 'em the door," Petey answered.

A high altitude spark shower appeared over the ridge. Cal called Avinash, "P3, what's your status?" Comm silence gave the response.

"This is P1," Denise said, "Three bogeys down but I'm bleeding fuel and luck. Need some landing coordinates."

Cal saw a transport in the flats unloading more troops, and he choked out, "Uploading your coordinates, P1. Happy landing. It has been an honor." A smoking blaze tore across the sky as twenty to thirty infantry, two new cannons, and the transport ship they arrived on were engulfed in Denise's fireball landing.

Angela flew by the house followed by two fighters. The closest got a beam of light shot through it's canopy cutting the craft through to the tail. The second craft swerved from the phase cannon so Petey could only cut off one wing causing it to spin into the base of the ridge. A weeping Angela said, "Sorry friends, I'm no good to you now. Gotta hang up my dancing shoes." She flew off toward the settlement.

The homing device on Cal's skimmer got him home safely after many late drinking sessions. He'd wake up when the heat overcame his delirium, safely parked outside his house. Now the skimmer was right where it was needed. Cal laid on the dusty ridge with a view of the front of his home. Small arms fire and an occasional electron rifle bolt from the windows hit different targets throughout the fight. Cal pulled his hand held and set off a high pitched squealing from the skimmer.

All shooting from the house stopped. Crashing and swearing could be heard inside, and then mercs came scrambling over furniture and out the door and windows. Cal's electron bolts burned them down one by one.

Silence took over the valley. Cal called out, "GS2 report."

Petey called back, "I'm good, but alone. Nothing moving on my screen."

"GS3 report."

"GS3 is gone. WS1 hit bad. No visual," Wing Lu said.

Cal called to Angela, "P2 report."

"Any landing you walk away from, right?" Angela responded.

Cal's front door burst open again and a mountain of a pig squeezed through the door frame squealing and tearing up the bodies on the ground. Cal shouted, "Hold fire. He's a friendly ... just don't get too close for a few hours."

Cal switched off his shield and yelled, "Trevor, put the body down!"

Chapter 8 - Cheers to the Fallen

"Three th-things you should know about p-pigs."

"What's that?" Petey said.

"They're smart," Cal said, "and their l-l-loyal."

Wing Lu, propped up in a corner table with his head wrapped over one eye said, "That's only, only two things, Cal."

"Huh? Oh, the th-third thing is ... yeah, they s-smell good."

"What!? Are you crazy?" Petey said, "Angela, no more for Cal. Cut him off!"

Wing said, "You been living with 'em too long mate."

Cal waved his massive arms, "No, no, no! I mean they h-have good smellers, g-g-good noses. If you hurt them they remember, and they can sniff you out."

Angela behind the bar asked over the confusion, "Cal, did the boy get out alive?"

"Andrew? Oh yeah, r-right as light," Cal said. "He h-holed up with Sybil in the t-tunnel. Mercs didn't even kn-know he was there."

The doorlock opened and a dusty Avinash announced, "I see I am too late to buy the first drinks."

"Avi!" Petey said, "You sneaky bugger! How come you didn't report in?"

Avinash hooked a thumb at a new customer coming through, "You can blame her, Captain Jack."

The tall, dark haired woman stepped through looking calm and in charge. She looked about and walked straight to Cal's table. He and Petey attempted to stand.

"You better remain seated there Sergeant Workman. You're looking a bit wobbly. I came to say thank you. You said it wouldn't kill me to say it. Came damn close."

Avinash jumped forward, "Her ship took out two of the big birds. She tractored me in under comm silence. I couldn't answer you."

"Captain J-Jack?" Cal asked thumping awkwardly down in his seat.

The captain said, "That was the thanks you asked for. Now for the please. Please may I have a brew?"

Petey called out, "Angela, a cold one for our new friend, on Cal's bill."

The doorlock spun open again and the younger crewman named Jamie entered and said, "Captain, we are loaded and prepped."

Captain Jack said, "I need to wing out folks, but you know the mercs will be back in greater numbers, more gear. Their reputation is at stake, and a freighter load of money on the line. I can offer all of you a lift or a job. I've seen you in action. I could use your skills and discipline."

Wing Lu said, "I'm a little off my game Cap. Not sure I'd be much use."

Captain Jack looked his way and said, "We can sort out some of the issues if you are willing."

Wing Lu lifted his glass, "I got no more prospects here. I'm in."

Petey said, "I stick with my mates, fire or rain."

Angela asked, "Jobs doing what?"

The captain looked her in the eye, "You would fly fighters and train younger pilots. I also need someone to oversee the maintenance kit. The rest we can sort out on the fly."

Angela said, "Don't feel like ending my ride here, but like Petey said, I'm with my mates."

The captain looked to Cal, "Avinash has already agreed if you all agree. We are all waiting on you, Sergeant."

Petey said, "It's what you wanted, Cal, being a team again." Cal had gone quiet but now looked up at the captain, "For my m-me and my m-mates, it's not s-safe here. I have s-some l-loose ends, but I think we sh-should sign up."

Petey handed the captain a beer, and she lifted it and said, "To fallen mates." Glasses raised and drunk.

The captain raised her glass again and said, "Harry Bolger!"

All joined in, "To Harry!"

Chapter 9 - We Signed Up for What?

"Does it matter so much?" Captain Jack asked while calculating course stages for the armored freighter. "A mercenary invasion was your alternative. You probably saved the lives of everyone you know on Cardea."

Cal filled up a large part of available space on the small bridge. Feet apart and unmoving he said, "Some of my b-best and w-worst decisions came from from the b-bottom of a mug, but I still need to know. I ass-assume you know."

"You're with your mates, the ones left."

"Been l-listening, have you? D-Dodging the question only makes my n-need greater."

Jack said, "First jump, hang onto something." Captain pushed a button causing red lights and an alarm to sound. Cal felt the vibration of distant metal grinding open followed by a murky glow in front of the ship disrupting star light ahead. The ship sailed into the glow, shuddering and shaking. Cal heard the angel song in his head, high tingling voices making indecipherable sounds followed by a violent jolt as the ship exited the portal created by the quantum generator.

Cal wiped the tears he always got. "Are you well, Sergeant," Captain asked.

"Angel song. Where are we h-headed and why?" He demanded.

Captain Jack said, "Now that we are out of the Coelus system we are safer from mercs for the moment. Jamie, status. Katrina, scan?"

A shy face peaked around a large screen, "Minimal debris, Captain. Navigating minus three, plus one point six two." Cal's gaze caused Katrina to retreat again.

Jamie's voice came over the comm, "Lights all green. Rechecking lander tie downs."

"I am the captain. If you don't want to walk home you'll follow orders without question."

Cal matched her tone and directness, "Want to be the c-captain? I w-want you to be the captain. But, captain, s-somethings are worth dying for, putting your m-mates at risk for. Somethings are n-not. Do you f-follow orders blindly?"

Captain Jack stood up facing the hulk unblinking, "Yes, I do, and so will you."

Their eyes locked, and Cal felt an intense connection. He said with growing awareness, "M-Maybe you d-do, but not this time. You're c-conflicted. If, if you are doing this to impress someone. It won't work."

Violent emotions rose to the surface as Jack looked away breaking the connection. "Get off my bridge! Now!"

"Aye captain, for now."

Chapter 10 – Background

Below Cal told his mates, "C-Captain's not saying y-yet, but she will."

Angela sitting across the galley table said, "She hasn't locked down the weapons. If she felt threatened, that'd be her first move."

Wing Lu rubbed the scar starting on his forehead continuing underneath his eyepatch and onto his cheek said, "Benefit of the doubt for now, but the clock is humming."

"What about the fighter bay!" Avinash said excitedly.

Angela agreed, "First class state of the art craft. Whatever we are, we are well funded. These pilots are green as grass though. Don't get attached."

Cal asked, "What's the c-crew count?"

"Calculating our odds, Cal?" Petey asked.

"Always."

Angela said, "Four pilots, twelve mechs. I've seen six general maintenance, probably infantry on the side."

"No spec guards," Wing Lu said, "Bit of a surprise there."

Cal said, "Bridge crew, I count f-four, m-make that five. Just saw a pretty f-face up there."

Angela squinted, "Pretty face, Caleb? Not the captain?"

Cal frowned, "A new f-face. S-Satisfied?"

Avi and Wing shared smirks, Angela shook her head and said, I hope this ends better than last time."

Petey asked, "What happened last time?"

Cal ignored them saying, "That makes twenty seven crew plus five of us. There's births for 120. Three shifts makes transport for 360. Secret mission or rendezvous for more crew?"

The captain walked through the door. All eyes turned, but no one stood, no salutes. Remnants of strong emotion still churned under her surface, eyes red, shoulders and arms tensed. The captain said, "No time for pep talks, straight to the point. I need your help. I was not on Cardea to say thanks. I am headed for the Achlys system."

Breathing in the room stopped.

Angela said, "Why were you on Cardea?"

"The first time, when Cal helped me, I was there to retrieve archives from your unit's action on Onyx."

Wing Lu said, "All information was sent to home planet. Why bother?"

Jack replied, looking at Angela, "Much of it was erased. What remains is locked down by Information Ministry. I needed the original source memory."

Wing Lu asked the big question, "Why are you doing this? What is the point?"

"Pieter LaBura is the point, head of the Allied party and the new government. The other parties are scared he will expose their corruption. They are correct, he will. He intends to."

"So Cardea ..." Angela prompted.

"Your action on Onyx, the ghost town of Travertine specifically, was to prevent the Scythians from taking control of the temple."

Wing Lu said, "After we pulled back you bombed a shit storm on it. Pile of rocks now, very small rocks."

Captain Jack said, "We didn't know why Scythians were so far into Confed space. Their sole purpose was possession of the temple. They started with a secret scouting mission, a single transport. We captured three of them. Suddenly, an armada is invading along the entire quadrant. You were ordered to Travertine. Harry's sacrifice made them withdraw. The rest you know."

Cal said, "Yeah, Harry along with Bendara, Sally, Weasel, Umpqua, the whole first core replacements transport ..."

Avinash added, "His name was Anthony. He hated being called Weasel."

Wing Lu said, "He earned the nick."

"But why the temple? The ruins are destroyed," Angela said trying to keep focus.

Captain said, "The temple was ancient, but was built on carved stones even older. The prisoners we captured were scientists, not soldiers. They were working on a new portal technology, planet based. Also, we didn't bomb the temple. All their forces in the tunnels underneath were dead. Only the abandoned town was destroyed."

"But we never got to the temple," Cal said, "and we were the forward unit."

"Scans showed no life after the battle. We interrogated the prisoners after the battle. The scientists saw their mates violently cut down all around them before capture, but they never saw an attacker or weapon. The three survivors had their brains stretched thin about it."

Angela shook her head saying, "What does this have to do with Pieter LaBura and Travertine?"

"A powerful creature attacked premier LaBura. It was invisible. Blasters had no affect. I stopped it with a sword. The DNA test on my blade found no blood, only a trace of Agridot, a crystal found on Onyx."

So you're taking a crew of thirty to fight off a new Scythian hoard over some new portal tech?" Wing Lu asked.

"Hoard?" Captain said, "Smaller than a hoard. Could be troop size or larger., and whatever the technology, Scythians were willing to gamble an all out war to get it."

Chapter 11- Prep Time

"How many revs until Onyx?"

Cal, pulled up his considerable weight in multiple repetitions to overhead bars in the gym, a side room to the fighter bay, and wheezed out, "Ten revs (whoosh) better get some (whoosh) water and rest (whoosh)."

Listening in from the weight bench Jamie asked, "What's Onyx like?"

Petey said, "Never been. Heard it's like Cardea but windier. Atmo isn't too bad, gravity a bit less. Some O2, but you need nose tubes or you get headaches. From the stories I'm expecting high orbit bomb craters everywhere."

Angela walked in wearing a pink sports bra, camo trousers and boots, hair in a high pony tail. She tossed her towel over a wall rail and started stretching.

"Were you on Onyx?" Jamie asked.

Angela said, "No, Petey and I were replacements after Onyx. Avinash too. Only Cal and Wing Lu are left of the originals."

A maintenance crewman asked, "How many engagements for the unit?"

Cal lay down on a pad and said, "Twenty t-two."

Eyes popped and jaws dropped.

Petey added, "He's not even counting post invasion clean up, dozens of quick deploys, and the three scrapes since furlough. Most decorated unit in Confed. Burned through a hell of a lot of replacements. Avinash joined after the invasion. He's been through 18 dances. Angela and me only saw twelve of 'em. She's the only officer left."

Angela said, "That's why they call us the Honey Badgers. So when Cal or one of us politely asks you to do something ... you listen, you obey. You just might make it home."

One of the mechs murmured, "Honey Badgers, what a stupid name."

Petey said, "You think so, ace? Look up honey badger on the net. Most feared animal on any planet they been dropped. No fear, all aggression."

Cal stood and said, "Finish your w-work outs, clean your weapons, and h-hit the racks if you aren't on duty. And wash up. I d-don't want to s-smell you until I have to. Drink all the w-water you can hold. H-Helps with flight and gravitation lag."

Cleaning his equipment back in the dorm Cal remembered his conversations with Jack. Even angry, her skin glowed, so smooth, so flawless, Her hair, so jet black. Cleaning his kit Cal uncomfortably recalled feeling her emotions, "And what is this weird connection?"

Avinash walked out of the head drying off and said, "What did you say?"

"Nothing Avi. T-Talking to m-myself."

"I hope you're done, Cal. I need sleep."

Cal replayed the encounters with Jacquelin over and over as he washed, and again as he lay down. Eventually he forced his mind to shut down.

Chapter 12 – Like Old Times

His oblivion was interrupted by the stations alarm and red flashing light.

Cal swung out of his rack loudly proclaiming, "Saddle up gentlemen. Avi, I need you airborne as soon as we hit high atmo. Wing, what am I carrying for you?"

Wing Lu said, "Sitting next to your pack, mate. All set."

"Anyone moon bound, I want boots in the hangar in ten minutes. Move it!" The flurry of activity fell into the cadence of soldiers stepping double time toward freight elevators. Cal checked the sand and breathing gear for each of the eight landing team standing at ease on the flight deck.

Angela briefed the assembled team including Avinash and two other pilots, "No combat craft of any force on the scans, but we take no chances. Four G fighters precede the lander. Non deploy pilots are to stay belted in for 90 minutes. After that you can de-plane but stay close."

She turned to Cal, "Ten butts on the lander. Equipment is loaded. Coordinates are loaded in the buggy units and personal comm packs. Captain on deck!"

Pilots and soldiers snapped to attention as Captain Jack stepped off the elevator and marched to the front and said, "Simple steps ladies and gentlemen, we are setting down south of the city, half a click from the temple. Five to each sand buggy. Sergeant Workman will lead until we reach the temple. I lead from there. We are here to scout the tunnels under the temple for any sign of recent activity. We will secure the area, then seal the entrances upon exiting. Any questions?"

Wing Lu raised a hand, "Scans of the surface?"

"No human activity on the surface. None in the tunnels, but I have lost confidence in tunnel scans from orbit. Also, along with maps you have mineral analysis built into the comm scanners. Pilots are to give us cover to complete the mission. Any other questions? Okay, let's load up and get this done. Sergeant, you are with me."

The captain climbed into the lander's cockpit. Cal sat in the co-pilot seat.

Engines flared to life as oxygen evacuated from the bay. Outer seal slid open followed by the inner seal. Four G fighters hovered, then dropped into high atmo flying in recon patterns. The lander lifted and followed into the black.

"Out with it Workman," Jack said, "Are you going to follow orders or don't you like following a woman?"

Painful memories surged forward and Cal forced out, "L-Leaders fail you. They lose their n-nerve and make bad d-decisions. They lead you into traps. They g-get shot, and leave your m-mom to s-starve."

After an uncomfortable pause Captain Jack asked, "What about Harry, what did he ever do to you?"

"He l-left me behind."

Jack nodded to herself. Looking out the front shield she said, "Sergeant, I promise you, I won't leave you behind."

Cal felt the steel in her words and the bond was set. Then he asked, "Is that w-why the captain is deploying with troops, a s-suicide mission? You should h-have told us."

Jack watched the fighters thin trails and followed them down in the corkscrew journey to the surface. She said, "I'm the only one here experienced with this enemy."

"And n-no one knows you are h-here. We're off the b-books, off the radar."

Jack smirked, "Off the books, yes. I wish no one knew about this. Who ever was behind the attack on Pieter knew we would come here. If my guess is correct, they will be here shortly if not here already."

"So a suicide m-mission."

"Not if I can help it," she said through gritted teeth fighting the ship into the denser layers of atmosphere.

"But you kn-know who's coming. Wait, you said P-Pieter? You are ... c-close?"

"I've known him since primary school. Check the ground scan. We're headed toward the rocky hill between the town and the escarpment."

Switching to open comm, Jack said, "P1, report."

Angela reported back, "Scan is clear at surface, no heat signature, no shields. Tunnel openings on monitor show clear. Some magnetic flux, nothing drastic. What are we looking for?"

"I'll tell you when I see it."

Chapter 13 - Going Downtown

"P2, report."

Avinash replied, "No sign. I'm a little suspicious. There should be something, miners, scavengers, something."

"P3."

"Some landing blasts. Nothing recent. Atmo clear."

Giant boulders dwarfing the troop buggies showed evidence of cut flat surfaces and carved right angles partially buried providing evidence of ancient stonework, but now providing a shield from sandblasting wind.

Cal ordered, "Heading downtown in pairs. WS1 lead us into the tunnel.. Handing comm control to C1."

Wing Lu moved forward slow walking with one of the grunts following him. Low glow scan images hovered in front of their faces, enhancing terrain and guiding them.

The captain said, "G3, G4 secure entrance. If we lose comm you're the relay to the sky."

Wing Lu, switched from rifle to pistol, and led through a tilted, but smooth triangular opening in the rock face of the ridge leading the team into the dark.

Cal felt cool stillness brush his face at the end of the triangle tunnel formed by massive stones he now saw were perfectly mated. There were no gaps between the rock slabs even though the joints were not straight. Cal walked hunched even though the cave was well over his head.

The captain asked, "WS1, any life forms?"

"Algae, and here is someone's hand. It's been sliced at the wrist. Scythian uniform bits. G1 is hyper-venting."

Captain said, "G3 status."

"Good Cap."

"Mind your manners. G1, head to the surface and replace G3."

Petey said, "GS1 moving in behind lead. Big ol' garage or hangar down here, Skipper. Come on down and check your IR."

Cal switched to infrared as he entered the high cavern. Areas on the cavern wall showed faint heat glow along seams and fissures. The four soldiers ahead shone brightly, Jamie hurrying toward him wanted to say something but Cal cut him off and waved him past, "Talk about it later."

Cal and the captain turned off infra and shined lights into the heights above. Wing Lu said, "Three more tunnels lead out of here plus smaller cracks and fissures, got 'em covered. What's the call C1?"

Petey asked, "What do ya make of this thing?"

Lights shone on a smooth section on the right side of the cavern wall perpendicular to the floor. The sloping ceiling and wall had been cut into a large, glass smooth vertical doorway three meters tall and wide. Inside the smooth surface was another shallow rectangular doorway. The interior of the door was as smooth as the outer surface. The depth of the door was only a body width.

Petey said, "Looks like a door to no where."

"Focus people. Not why we're here," Cal said.

The Captain said, "We'll start from the left. WS1, take the left tunnel With G3. GS1 take center with M1. I'll take G2 with me on the right. Watch for any sign, floor, artifacts, someone took a piss, anything."

Cal said, "M2, you're with me. We'll monitor comm from between the two boulders in the center."

A few minutes later Wing Lu whispered, "Left tunnel, a lot of blood, drag marks. Probably bodies ahead. Walls narrowing, it's getting colder."

"Center tunnel sloping down, some odd ledges different sizes on our right wall."

Captain Jack said, "Right tunnel multiple footprints, signs of small gathering. Small quartz crystals in pockets."

Mech 2 monitoring comm said, "Orbit sees G1 and 4 with comm, S1 and M2 visible no comm, GS1 fading in and out. No one else."

Wing Lu said, "No bodies yet but some cool blue green crystals. Scan says quartz with agridot mixed in."

The captain said, "Get some samples, biggest you can find."

"They're anchored in rock. I'll have to blast them out."

Captain replied, "No blasting. Use your knife." As if reading Wing's mind she added wryly, "I'll buy you a new one."

Wing chuckled, putting the point of a large knife under the edge of a formation. He hit the pommel with his palm. No effect except to dull the point. Several attempts only further blunted the weapon. In frustration, Wing put the point into the middle of a large formation and used a rock to strike the knife. No affect on the first strike but the second strike broke out chunks of pointed white crystals with blue and purple points. In the big cavern Cal spun to the right, interrupter leveled. Something had moved in his peripheral sight.

Wing said, "C1, I got a few points. They're pretty."

"Get a few more," C1 said.

Cal took a careful step toward the doorway. The sound of Wing's knife registered in his ear piece and the doorway surface shimmered like troubled water and stopped. Cal reached out a hand and felt the smooth stone unyielding.

Cal called, "GS1, hit your knife again."

The knife rang out. Cal's hand was ready. Suddenly, at his touch the cavern disappeared and he was in something like a dense fluid. He reached to switch his breathing tube to ... to nothing. Cal felt no oxygen debt, no panic to breathe. It was not light but he could see what looked like eddies in the gel surrounding him, like trails of bubbles curving, twisting off in directions high, low left and right. Some were faint, some clear, some were wide, some thin, leading always around and away from an area of ultimate black. The black seemed to pulse, and pull at him.

Cal turned to face trails near him. Any path he focused on caused images to flash across his mind. One clear trail leading around behind him gave images of the cavern he just left. Cal turned to follow it and found himself staring back into the cave. A man dressed in black stood next to M2 monitoring comm in a crouch between boulders, unaware of the presence. The man pulled a heavy knife and before Cal could react the knife stabbed down into M2's neck between body armor and helmet. M2 slumped to the ground while the man walked toward the left tunnel where Wing Lu investigated.

Cal furiously fought against whatever surrounded him and stopped. A man dressed in colorful clothes with a gold, close fitting head cap stepped out of the depths close to the doorway. Cal froze. The colorful man held a hand up in peace. He reached out a bare arm, and lightly pulled Cal's arm into the direction of the clear trail. Cal was jerked forward into the cavern, but the light was different and sound had ceased. He ran down the left tunnel dodging protrusions in time to see G3 drop to the floor. Wing whipped around with an electron rifle, the beam slicing through the man in black with no effect. A trace hit Cal's arm. Feeling nothing, Cal streamed forward. Wing backing down the tunnel firing and drawing his knife. Cal slammed into the man in black driving him into the tunnel wall and down to the floor.

The man twisted to the side, hurt but not stopped, he slashed at Cal and then lunged for Wing, his knife falling short as Cal grabbed an ankle pulling him back.

"Wing, get back!" Cal tried to shout, causing the man in black to roll over with a smile and slide past and through Cal and vanish.

Chapter 14 – What's What

Wing continued firing sporadically, maximizing energy pack life. Cal's attempts to talk to him had no affect. Cal crouched back up the tunnel guessing the beams wouldn't hurt him but still reacting from training and experience.

The stone door was smooth and solid but he could see the trail of his previous passage next to the door. Following his own trail he passed through the wall and behind the door. No colorful man was in sight. Cal looked into the depths in many directions. The black area throbbed with trails leading away from it, but nothing else moved. He approached the back side of the stone door. Stepping through the portal he was immediately facing the door. Cal turned in time to see M2's head twist and blood spurt as he fell to the floor. Cal immediately heard Wing's call for backup and heard the sizzle of the electron beams in the left passage.

The silence was broken by Wing calling, "What the hell just happened? G3 is down. Something attacked but disappeared. I never saw it."

Captain Jack dashed into the cavern while Wing continued to fire sporadically. M2 convulsed while Cal stared.

The captain rushed in and demanded, "S1, report!"

Cal completed his full description of events as he experienced them. G1 and 4 remained in place above while the rest assembled near the smooth door..

"Easy enough to test," Petey said, "strike the crystal again."

"WS1, pull out a crystal and your knife," Captain Jack said. "Give the crystal a tap." Wing complied. All eyes on the door saw no change.

"Hit it harder," Captain said. Again, no change in the door.

"Try chipping an edge," Cal said.

Wing put a crystal on the floor. Putting the knife at the edge, he struck the back of the blade with a rock. A small flake flew off and the doorway turned liquid.

Captain called out, "No one touch it! S1, describe the man in black, clothes, shoes, skin, hair, everything."

"Almost as tall as me, but thinner, white skin, wavy brown hair, stylish cut to it. Shoes weren't shiny. Trousers loose fit and one of those shirts with the wrap around chest."

"You mean a military button over."

Cal said, "Yeah, the button over, but too tight for military."

Captain continued, "And the man with the gold cap?"

"He wore a robe but no shirt, with a long skirt. The clothes had designs on 'em, in all different colors. Now that I think of it, he had a thick gold necklace and a gold disk with designs on it."

The captain sighed, "None of this makes sense. We need to keep looking for clues." Turning to Cal she said, "S1, our only partial defense is for you to stand watch inside the door. Take a crystal just in case."

Wing pulled a long handled knife, "This will give you an edge in a knife fight." Wing pushed a release next to the hilt and the handle extended twice it's length. Wing Lu showed Cal the release button, and pushed the blade back down. Cal smiled and tucked the blade into his belt.

"We'll continue searching the tunnels. G4, pair up with WS1. G1, you'll maintain comm from the surface. Can you handle that?"

"Yes Cap ... , uh C1," Jamie said inspiring confidence in no one.

Cal said, "I need a way to chip a crystal with one hand to use the door."

Wing said, "Crystal's not super hard. You just need to scrape it."

Cal scraped the crystal with a knife edge causing the shimmering but it stopped moving as he reached out to touch it. "Like I said, I need to do it with one hand."

Wing pulled out a thin file, shot it with his blaster heating it, then bent it in a circle around the rifle barrel. "The ring doesn't mean we're steady, and you owe me a new one."

Chapter 15 - Into the Labyrinth

Cal placed the file ring on, put his hand on the wall and scraped the crystal. The cave disappeared. Cal instantly faced two Scythian soldiers rushing at him with knives. He parried the first knife pushing the first soldier into the second forcing a downward stab from the second to miss. The first pulled another blade spinning and driving the point into Cal's stomach but stopping at the body armor. Cal pummeled the side of his face and drew the long handled knife. The second leaped over his falling comrade knife held high. Cal shoved his longer arm holding a longer handle and extended the blade into second soldier's chest with brutal force breaking rib bones as it penetrated.

The first Scythian reached into a pocket. Cal quickly skewered the wrist stepping down on his neck. The crushing step failed as the surface where they stood gave way. Cal fell with one knee onto the Scythian's chest and head slapped the soldier unconscious.

Seeing no other threats, Cal pulled the skewered wrist out of the pocket. Instead of a weapon Cal found a small metal case. The case had a plunger on one side and a hole on another with a crystal sliver sticking out. Cal pocketed the case. Turning to the cavern he stepped through. Everyone was watching him.

"It didn't work," the Captain said. "Try it again, S1."

"It did work," Cal said, "Look what I found." A dazed Scythian was dangling from Cal's grip. "There's a dead one on the other side, but I could only hang onto one. I'll go get him." Cal then realized he was missing the crystal Wing had given him. He pulled out the metal case taken from the unconscious soldier, and pushed the plunger with his hand on the wall. Cal immediately re-entered the portal and re-pocketed the case, drawing the knife.

The Scythian's body was gone. In it's place was the man in black laying face up, staring, his chest split open. Cal searched his pockets, looked for tattoos, checked his clothes and shoes.

Cal looked around. The only limit to the area was the undefined black space. He could not tell how far away it was, so no guess on how big, but he could feel it pulsing or swirling, small eddies moved out and back. The fluid around him wasn't thick any more, and he could see better than the first time. The surface where he was standing was solid until he pushed his hand down and felt the give. Cal clearly saw trails through the space, and guessed these were paths others had created since he had been pulled into one by the man with the gold cap. Each path he faced gave off hints of images and colors. Some felt old, ancient. Others were fresh with vibrant images.

Cal stepped into a wide path and was instantly back in the cavern he just left. Instead of his crew, Scythian soldiers worked, and what he guessed were scientists looking at instruments, paid no attention to him.

Looking over the shoulders of the scientists he could see Confed ships on their scanners. Panic flashed around the workers. Confederation ships had found them.

As they started packing up equipment the same two soldiers who attacked Cal earlier appeared in the tunnel coming down from the surface, time tripping like Cal. They started killing their own men.

Cal tackled the one he had captured. Cal pinned his arms and reached into his pocket. Drawing out the metal case from the soldier's pocket he knew would be there, he jammed it into the soldier's open mouth and pushed the button. The soldier disappeared.

The other one now aware of Cal's presence kept dodging around boulders as he continued his killing spree with a knife and metal club, running around the room. The scientists started panicking from the unseen nightmare, screaming as they ran here and there sometimes right into the soldier's blade or club. Cal finally trapped him in a corner, and said, "Gotcha," even though no sound came.

The Scythian reached into a pocket and disappeared like the other one.

Chapter 16 - The Torrent

"They were trying to cover up the reason for their presence," Captain Jack said adding, "What did you learn about the man in black?"

"Tattoo on his right shoulder had been removed. Nothing in his pockets. His shoes had no label, but they were made of animal hide top and bottom with shrink fasteners. A seam in the shirt had a name stitched in, South End, LTD, followed by the letters BA."

"Barnard Anders," the Captain said, "fine garments for fine gentlemen, a home world busker to the rich. Pieter is also a customer."

Jamie spoke frantically from top side, "C1, a large cruiser just dropped ten G fighters into atmo with no markings and no hailing. P1 is asking for engagement orders."

Captain Jack ordered, "Full engagement with combatants including cruiser if possible. Cal, I'm going inside with you."

Cal said to Wing Lu, "WS1, you'll be posted inside the door. We'll need to pull back to just this cavern and the mouth of the cave. GS1, M1, and G2 hold the cavern. G4 and G1 hold the opening, but retreat if necessary to the cavern.

Wing Lu held out a stone, "C1, you'll need a crystal. Scraping on steel is your best bet. We'll all need to activate our stone."

"Quick safety tip," Cal said, "Best avoid the black area inside the door."

Captain Jack tucked the crystal into an empty cartridge loop on her belt, put her blade tip at the ready and said, "Three hands up." Cal, the Captain, and Wing Lu placed hands on the door. "Three, two, one," she counted off quickly.

The world disappeared and traces of previous passages surrounding the central blackness faced the trio giving hints of the other end. Cal turned to explain but no words came from his open mouth. The Captain scanned the paths quickly. She gave a hand signal of two spread fingers pushed together as one and pointed at a path looping in a wide arch up, left, and behind. Cal held a knife up in the right hand and held his left hand out. Wing Lu and the Captain held up knives, but Wing

Lu stepped back close to the door. The Captain took Cal's hand and stepped into the path.

A flood of images, objects, doorways, and colors poured past them. Cal saw people in the images, some foreign, some in familiar military garb. Captain Jack pointed with her knife and moved out of the stream into an office littered with wounded and dead bodies of Allied Party security officers. A cleaner version of herself, Captain Jacquelin Jammula, dressed and pressed for parade, but looking frantic and standing with drawn sword next to a seated Premier Pieter LaBura who looked stunned. A movement caught Cal's attention. A momentary mirror reflection of a woman's face with a lock of red hair in an adjoining room.

Security forces burst through the door and swarmed into the offices oblivious of Cal and the dusty version of Captain Jack. The dusty captain shook her head at Cal. They held hands while Cal hit the plunger pulling them back into the torrent of silent images.

Chapter 17 – Second Verse

Jack jerked sideways as soon as she started their descent into time. She and Cal were in a darkened version of the same office space before any damage from the skirmish. The windows showed a sparkling city set off by dark skies.

Captain signaled with her flat palm forward and Cal moved to the nearest wall to watch. With nothing happening Cal opened a door to look around. An empty bathroom reminded him he need to pee when he was back in the cavern. In the bathroom he saw the mirror that would later reflect the face of an unknown woman sometime in the future.

Past the bathroom he saw a sliver of dim light from under another door. A sitting room lined with clothes racks and a communications center were inside. A bedroom lay beyond. Cal peaked in to find the dusty captain looking down at Pieter and the woman he had seen earlier. The captain's shoulders were heaving and eyes squeezed shut. Moved, Cal put a hand on the captain's shoulder. The captain led Cal through a hidden door back into main office where she slumped into a chair in the corner, head in her hands wracked with silent wailing. Cal, unable to speak outside the fabric of time, sat in an opposite corner watching the captain, unable to offer any comfort. Her weeping stabbed his soul in the dark. They sat disconnected and trapped outside time, accompanied only in their own thoughts and emotions.

Eventually the sky lightened. Hover vehicles in distant traffic streams now visible told of a city waking up. Lights came on under the door of the bathroom. The main office door opened for a cart with coffee and food wheeled in by a uniformed attendant who promptly left but another came in with papers and valise taking up a seat at a side desk. He sat but quickly looked up at the closed door bursting open. The dusty captain still sitting in the corner motioned to Cal to stay seated.

A man and woman stepped through firing multiple blaster bolts burning through the seated attendant. A side door opened revealing the uniformed Captain and another guard charging through and firing at the intruders, cutting down the man. The woman slipped sideways and fired hitting the guard in the torso knocking him backward. Additional security soldiers entered from the hallway weapons drawn.

Suddenly, two men in all black garb appeared in the middle of the room with knives in hand slashing at the arriving security. Bodies dropped and blood flew.

Cal and the captain, silent sentinels, rushed in from their corner seats. Cal recognized one of the men in black as the one he faced earlier. Cal saw the dusty Captain dodge a thrust and drive her knife home lifting her opponent off his feet. Cal and his enemy in black grabbed each other's wrists. It was not an even match as Cal's wrist was twice as thick.

Cal's superior position melted away as the man before him disappeared and reappeared behind him. Cal realized the brilliant tactic just before the blow to his head sent him sprawling. From the ground he saw the clean captain fighting with multiple Scythians when he hit his plunger ripping himself out of the office and zipping back to the cavern to see the time tripping Wing Lu tearing through attackers stuck in normal time. G2 was down. G4 and G1 were fighting hand to hand. Petey and M1 exchanged fire with additional forces in the tunnel.

Cal stood and leapt back up the path to the office fight. In the torrent he saw himself go down with the blow to the back of his head. He stepped out behind the man who just hit him. Cal shoved the man in black off balance, then turning, he grabbed the Captain's arm and hit the plunger. The two bounced down to the cavern door and immediately back up to the office reappearing on opposite sides of the ring of enemies throwing them into confusion as the Captain and Cal cut down four of them quickly.

The first man in black charged toward the back offices. The uniformed Captain had thrown away her blaster and pulled a ceremonial sword from the wall and swung it wildly while stepping into the invisible melee as her forces continued to be killed and maimed.

Cal stepped out of the fight and threw an arm around the uniformed captain's waist and threw her out of the way of several knife strokes. He saw her unfocused look of terror as she landed contrasted by the dusty captain's look of wonder at Cal. The looks vanished into memory as the fighting reasserted priority.

Remaining Scythians disappeared and started reappearing. Cal needed help. He hit his plunger and flew back to the cavern finding

Wing Lu in a desperate fight with two skilled time traveling antagonists.

Cal jumped into the cavern fight driving one attacker to the ground with his long knife piercing downward. The other was swept off his feet in the confusion Cal created. Wing Lu landed on him as the attacker hit the floor. Several lightning fast stabs to neck, eyes, and throat guaranteed the enemy would struggle no more. Cal grabbed Wing Lu's arm. They flew to the cavern door and ricocheted up to the office.

Wing Lu flew into the battle around the dusty captain. Cal appeared next to the black dressed adversary knocking him sideways away from a stunned looking clean captain. His foe vanished and Cal instinctively spun around only to have the man return to his side and stab downward at Cal's neck.

Cal lifted his arm to block the strike which entered shoulder muscle spurting blood.

Wing Lu and the Captain ran to surround the last intruder. Their foe evaporated and reappeared across the room, then again by the entrance, then between Cal and the clean captain flailing her sword. Cal grabbed his opponent's slashing arm with his good hand. The man in black slipped away, and resurfaced next to the door leading to the back rooms where the premier hid.

He flung open the door and a flash of gold and bright colors filled the opening. A long handled weapon with heavy curving blade at the top slashed down the front of the black shirt. Their foe looked at his black shirt at the gaping fissure opened down his torso before collapsing backward.

The gold capped man in the colorful robe strode forward with his primal weapon pointed at Cal. Cal threw up his hands. Wing Lu and the dusty Captain did the same. The blade receded and a bare arm reached an open hand toward Cal.

Cal slowly pulled the bronze box out and placed it in the open hand. The Captain got the crystal out of the cylinder holder on her belt and handed it over. Wing Lu followed in turn.

The ancient one tucked them in his waist band, grabbed Wing Lu's wrist and held it out to the Captain. The Captain took Wing's hand and reached her other hand out to Cal. Once the three were connected the ancient one grabbed Cal's other hand. With his free hand the old man took a crystal and reached over to the clean, uniformed Captain Jacquelin standing wide eyed holding her drawn sword out. He scraped the crystal on her blade and the torrent swept the office away replacing it with the space behind the stone doorway looking into the cavern.

Stepping through the watery stone opening Petey saw them and exclaimed, "Welcome travelers! Did we win? This is clear the weirdest day of my life."

Chapter 18 - Cleanup

Petey asked, "Well, did we win?"

The Captain said, "We won, and we lost so much," she said morosely, dust and dirt marking the tracks of her tears.

"Where's the man in black?" Wing asked.

Cal said, "When we came back he wasn't with us."

The Captain asked, "Has the ship checked in?"

"G1 reports the skies clear. We can transport as soon as we clean up everything here. Your prisoner is still alive. Not sure how he managed that with our visitors aiming more at him than us. All trussed up he still managed to dodge the bolts."

"Cal, you're bleeding all over my new cave," Petey said, "Let me clean that up, mate."

The Captain said, "We've lost all our crystal samples. No one touch the door if it moves. We're going down the left tunnel to get more crystals. Cal, stop bleeding and come with. Wing Lu too. The rest of you keep guard and check in with G1 again."

Petey said, "In a snap, Cap. Gotta stop this bloke's leaking," as he tied the first knot over the wound binder. A few more knots and Petey exclaimed, "There you go, Clumsy. You owe me a brew, and no picking up anything heavy for a while."

Cal said, "Need a minute first, Cap. Gotta pee."

The captain led down the tunnel near the crystals the captain looked back to make sure they were alone. Then she looked at the other two and removed her ear comm. Cal and Wing did the same.

"You know dangerous information from what you've seen. It could get you killed. It could get us all killed."

"Who was the man in black?" Cal asked, "Did you know him?"

"Maarten Vos, son of the Unity Party leader Ricart Vos. I accompanied Premier LaBura to his funeral two years ago. His casket was open but he had a flag draped up to his neck. Swear to me you won't report any of this or even talk about it."

"We give our word, Cap," Wing said.

Cal said, "You were in love with him, with the Premier."

Involuntary tears reappeared. The captain calmly said, "In school my best friend and I fell in love with the same wonderful boy ... a long time ago. She won. She was good with people, good at hospitality, a perfect partner for a leader. I was good at hurting people. He was so perfect, so honorable, so upstanding. I never loved another man. I loved my friend too, and wouldn't come between them, but she knew ... she knew. It drove us apart."

The Captain turned to go.

"She is not as beautiful as you," Cal stammered, finally having words.

The captain turned back and said, "That was not his wife. WS1, you lead."

Wing Lu pointed to the old blood trails black against the stone. They followed the blood past the crystal samples and found a pile of bodies, ancient skeletons with many recent Scythian soldiers on top, and one man in all black clothing laid on top. Behind the bodies, in a carved out alcove, a tall skeleton wrapped in colorful cloth and a close fitting gold cap on his skull was propped up by a long handled curved axe.

After a stunned silence Cal said, "He was the guardian of the door."

Captain Jack said, "He needed help so he summoned us."

"Do we need more crystals?" Wing asked.

"No,"she said replacing her ear comm. "This is the captain. We are done here, folks. Get the prisoner ready for transport. On the lander in 15 minutes."

Leaving orbit Angela said, "Petey, you think you had a weird battle? I got shot down twice only to find myself back in the air trailing the ship that had been behind me."

Avinash said, "I was closing in on the transport bridge when I saw red splash their portals. The ship veered out of orbit ditching the fighters. Why would they do that?"

Petey asked, "So what did the travel team find behind the stone door?"

Cal quickly said, "We found Scythians. They were hiding behind the door."

"You saw a man in black," Jamie said.

"He was with the Scythians," Wing said. "All dead now."

Jamie followed with, "And the man with the gold hat?"

"Same, all dead," Cal said looking at Wing who nodded agreeing, "All dead."

"What about the door," Angela asked.

"Buried," Jamie said, "You didn't know? We bombed the temple just before we left orbit."

Petey said, "Chalk up another action for the Badgers. We only lost three on this turn."

Katrina poked her head into the galley with a worried look and said, "Cal, the captain would like a word. She's in the hold."

Cal said, "Be there in f-five, Kat."

After she left Wing Lu said, "She's a better choice than either of the Welkers. Good move, mate."

Cal said, "The captain? She's g-got all those f-female parts, but her eyes are the most d-dangerous."

Angela said, "Deep waters there, Sergeant. Step carefully."

Petey said, "Wait! You knew the Welkers? Both of them? That is so not fair!"

Cal, rising from his seat, sadly said, "No P-Petey, I really didn't."

Chapter 19 - Hold Please

"C-Captain?" Cal's baritone stammer boomed through the cavernous hold of the DS class freighter. He walked further in among the landers and fighters tied down securely. No maintenance crew were about. A vicious, heart rending cry made Cal jump. He walked carefully toward the trailing wail. In the middle of spare part crates he found the captain sitting on the deck, her back against an old thruster, strands of black hair pasted across the damp of her smooth coppery face.

Cal slid over a sturdy carton and sat his bulk down. No words. Like a friend he sat, silently guarding her private desolation of soul for as long as she needed. Time has no meaning in sorrow.

Hiding behind her hands Jacquelin gulped air and said, "I can't go back, Cal, and I can't go forward. Back on Onyx (sniff) you asked me if

I was on a suicide mission. Truth is, it was a suicide mission. I just didn't know."

"But you s-survived," Cal pointed out.

"Temporarily. There were always rumors. After all we had been through I didn't believe them. Getting put out or quitting the Allied party only brings the Unity and Treaty party operatives around for their pound of flesh, along with Central Security, and Information Security, some military," she added with a distraught, teary smile, "I've made a few enemies. And now I've pulled you and the rest of the crew down with me." Tears started anew.

"Then d-don't quit."

" Premier LaBura," she sneered, "has sold out his wife. He sold out his party, and his dream. Now he has sold me. I'm nothing in comparison."

Cal said, "The red h-head we saw him with is n-nothing. Women probably throw th-themselves at him all d-day long. Even the b-best man is tempted to cheat."

"Don't you understand?" Jack stormed, "The red head wasn't some bimbo off the street! That was Laurel Vos, daughter of the Unity party emir! She's the messenger! If she is fucking him the deal is already done! .... was done a long time ago. And I've killed us all ..." Quiet crying accompanied the last remnants of Jacquelin's hopes turning rancid.

After a bit Cal stood and said, "Cap, we might have another option. Give me a bit to figure this out, okay?" No response from the down turned face gave Cal permission to run off through the cases.

After the thunder of his strides faded and despite promises, Captain Jack screamed into the space above, "You idiot, you shithead! You wasted your whole damn life following this asshole!" Trailing off she said, "What a waste ... and I've killed the all the people dumb enough to follow me ... they'll go after father and my brother ... friends, anyone who would defend me ..."

More wailing followed.

Returning with Cal, Angela said, "Captain, Cal told us your situation, our situation. We also can't go back to Settlers Grove. Our plan is to acquire a ship and keep on the move. You could join us."

Captain Jack looked up through a riot of hair and said, "In my world the cost of failure is everything, everyone I have loved, all those dear to me will be dishonored, brutalized, raped, killed ... to cause me the most pain before they start on me." She continued to drone without looking up, "My father, doesn't even know what I do." A brief sob shook her followed by a gulp of air. Then looking up she said, "Thanks, but the least I can do is die fighting."

Cal said, "I'd r-rather die in Settlers Grove pub with mates all around me having a brew, but that's not going to happen."

Angela waited for the captain to catch her breath, then said, "If you can't go back, and you can't go forward, then change the rules. Find a reason for the Premier to need you."

The captain tilted her tear soaked face up again and said, "I've already been ordered to bring the prisoner from Onyx back to the capitol."

"Let's give him a reason to change the ... Wait, how did they know you had a prisoner?" Angela asked.

"I told them," Jack said, then thinking she said, "No, they already knew. They asked about prisoners."

Cal said, "Everyone on the sh-ship knows about the prisoner. O-Only three people kn-knew about the other one, and I just t-told Angela."

Wing Lu said, "I think we need to go talk to the living prisoner."

Chapter 20 – The Scythian

"Give me knife," the Scythian said with his chained hand held out to Cal.

The captain nodded and Cal pulled his large blade and handed it over. The Scythian cut open his pant leg and inserted the tip into the skin of his thigh. Wincing he popped a bloody lump out and handed it to Cal.

"A gift," the Scythian said, "Is tracer. Maybe they know I am here."

Angela asked, "How could they know? This tracer can't transmit interstellar. The ship would have to transmit the signal."

Wing Lu said, "Maybe the tracer uses a Confederation protocol, but Scythia would have to intercept the signal or maybe the ship's comm has a virus to send the signal without reporting it."

Captain Jack said, "It doesn't matter if it's intercepted or a virus. Someone in our government knows about the signal and what it means."

The Scythian returned the knife, handle first, to Cal then raised his eyebrows and said, "Someone ees talking to Scythian military command."

"How do we turn it off?" Captain Jack asked.

"Simple. Smash."

Cal dropped the tracer, and kneeling, hammered it with the pommel of his knife, spreading the shards and blood apart.

"Why would you help us?" Captain asked.

"I want to live longer. As prisoner, I am traitor. If I go back, slow death. I can help, and I can make Samogon."

"You would sell out Scythia?" Angela asked.

"Do you know what I love? I love my mother's cooking. I love when sun goes down over seas on Scythia home world. I would love to see family again. I think all these lost to me. What else can I do?"

"What were your orders?" Angela asked.

"Kill premier LaBura. He would be in back room. My commander get new orders to also kill big man," here he pointed to Cal, "then we get more new orders to go back and kill scientists long time back."

Angela shook her head and asked, "How did you get orders?"

"Officer met us inside door. It hurts brain to think about, yes?"

Chapter 21 - Change in the Wind

"Orders Captain?" Kat asked as the group from the brig entered the bridge.

The captain wiped her eyes again and smoothed her hair back, "Set a course for Wellington space dock in the Coelus system. This ship and crew are returning to Andromeda station as promised. To Angela she said, "We can't trust this Scythian."

"Why?" Cal asked, "He's been m-more truthful than anyone else we've b-been dealing with."

Angela said, "Truth is his best play to stay alive, but we can work with that."

Wing Lu said, "And he can make Samogon." Confused looks all around prompted Wing to add, "Scythian moonshine."

"I s-say we keep him alive," Cal said.

Captain Jack shook her head, "No, we can't afford him talking. He knows too much about the portal, about our security, and other state secrets. I want him and the other refuse incinerated before the jump. I'll tolerate no questions, no discussion. Move out and report to me as soon as you are done."

Shocked and angry looks punctuated the silence. Cal grit his teeth and turned to leave. Jack ordered, "Sergeant Workman, you will salute me!"

Cal threatened, "You're the c-captain, but you're not m-my captain." Two salutes later the three exited her presence.

The captain brooded, then rose to leave and told Kat tersely, "I need to talk to the maintenance chief. Watch the monitors. Make sure they comply."

Jamie stood square shouldered in front of Cal who was dragging the prisoner through the hold. Captain Jack watched from the maintenance chief's office one floor above the deck

Taking a fighting stance Jamie said, "No, I won't let you do this!"

The Scythian pled for mercy, wriggling in the grasp of Cal in the middle of the equipment stacks, heading toward the incinerator chute.

Angela stepped around him, stared dead pan at the young maintenance engineer and said darkly, "If you touch your weapon your last breath comes before you hit the deck. We've got orders. Step aside."

She offered no comfort, no reason. She gave two options, full compliance or oblivion. Jamie stood on the razor's edge, wavering between conscience and survival. Three hardened combat professionals, trained experienced killers faced him. He stepped aside shaking his head and saying, "This is wrong, what you are doing is wrong." The Scythian thrashed as much as his chains allowed. Jamie looked up to Captain Jack, then sprinted for the stairs.

Before Jamie reached the office door everyone heard Cal roar, "Enough!" Captain Jack and Jamie watched Cal lift the bound Scythian by the neck, choking him, then throwing his body to the floor amid the parts and crates. Wing Lu produced an equipment duffle and Cal tossed the limp body into the bag out of the Captain's sight. Angela and Wing lifted the dead weight up to the incinerator chute. Captain Jack called out the open office window, "Stop right there, Angela! I want someone to check that bag!"

A mechanic close by the chute looked up. The captain ordered him, "Look inside the bag. make certain there is a Scythian in it!"

The mechanic tentatively stepped up. Cal, red with anger, glared up at the captain. Wing Lu unzipped the canvas and the mechanic looked inside. He nodded up to Captain Jack who commanded, "Proceed," and she then turned back to her conversation with the chief. Jamie watched the bag slide in. The chute door closed with a decisive metallic thud.

Afterwards Cal, Wing Lu, Angela, Avinash, and Petey, the last of the Honey Badger unit, stayed in quarters talking quietly, complaining loudly, and avoiding contact with any others. The rest of the crew were happy to give them a wide berth.

Chapter 22 – Back on Cardea

The quantum hop was uneventful. Cal always heard angel song when passing through a quantum tunnel, a chorus of high tingling voices making indecipherable sounds. This time Cal heard the angel song in his dreams.

Automated docking at the orbiting station above Wellington Space Port set off mooring lights and sirens inside the freighter. Cal stormed past the captain refusing her the offer of conversation and salute as he walked to the airlock.

Jamie said, "Captain, you should have him thrown in the brig!"

The captain twisted a disbelieving look at Jamie, "Who is going to throw him anywhere? Besides, I need him."

The captain said to Angela, who did return her salute, "He can't stay here."

"Neither can any of us," Angela replied, "I'll talk to him. How are you getting back to home world?"

"I have to go planet side to report in. I'll arrange something there."

Wing Lu walked past with Petey and Avinash, all saluting. Petey said, "Don't worry about Cal, Captain. He's happy to go die on his pig farm."

Borrowing a freight tugger from Barney, the station manager, Cal rode out to the ridge above his old pig and nitrogen farm. As always, Lares met him at the door.

"I hope you aren't here to take back your farm, Cal. Nathan and his new bride are enjoying themselves down there."

"Good on 'em," Cal said and handed Lares a thick stack of papers covered in hand written notes, "Here, I b-brought a p-present."

"You Pirate! Where did you score all these ship numbers!"

"I've had s-some waiting in my h-hand held, but the bulk I got from a freighter's log, a freighter used by s-security and military."

Lares' eyes lifted conspiratorially, "A freighter from Andromeda's main station."

"That's right. P-Pirate yourself," Cal laughed and added, "A-Actually Lares, that's w-why I need to talk to you." Lares' friendly smile turned south.

Cal said, "Sh-Ships are giving off signals the captain and c-crew don't know about, tracking, tracing s-signals."

"How did you find out? You want me to tell you how to read them."

Cal said, "A Scythian p-prisoner in the brig. I g-got up close and p-personal until he was d-down right chatty. We found a tracer inserted into him."

"I didn't need to know that, Cal. This is why I left."

Cal squinted, "Then I'm g-guessing you're reading these ships to know if y-you're found out."

"Spin round, Cal. See your valley down there. Kind of a big circle."

"M-More like an oval."

Lares said, "With the hard pan on the valley floor my drone in low stationary orbit uses the valley like an antenna. Speaking of drones, mercenaries are watching Wellington and Shepherds Church for any sign of you."

Alarmed Cal said, "Are they c-close by?"

"If they are broadcasting off planet they're on the far side of Cardea," Lares said as he scribbled a note on an edge of paper he tore off and handed to Cal. "This is the vault where you'll find some tools for the work. The password is my wife's name followed by the coordinates of my drone. You best leave now and keep low."

Chapter 23 - Unstable

To Angela Barney the port commander said, "A ship, huh. You didn't hear this from me but the mercenaries you fought left a freighter in orbit and some G craft in the government hangar. There's also a bundle of equipment buried around outside of town. They didn't have enough pilots after your team gutted 'em," Barney said hobbling back to the main offices from the inbound terminal with his normal limp.

"This won't come back on you, will it?" Angela asked.

Barney said, "On me? Not likely. Those mercs showed up with a bad attitude, no reservations, no authorization for transporting hardware, the more of their crap ya take outta here the better I'll like it. You can tell Cal the same."

Petey said, "Thanks Barney, we'll take as much as we can carry."

Barney gave Petey a withering glare. "It's Major Wisener to you! Not another word, Private!" Petey shrunk back behind Avinash who also looked annoyed at him.

The ground exploded to their left and then in front of them. All fell to the hard pan surface and drew any weapons they had. The G fighter banked and swung around for another pass.

All heard in their ear pieces, "Angela! Angela! Mercs still have presence here.! Don't go out in the open!"

Behind sheets of hard pan torn up by previous blasts Angela said, "Too late, Cal. Their on us. What's your ETA?"

"Almost to the first checkpoint," Cal shouted pushing the tugger to its limit, the wind rushing past him.

"Come in hot. We're going high comm 216." Turning, she repeated to those behind her, "High comm 216," and saw Wing and Avinash dragging Barney to cover leaking a red trail. Plasma bolts started burning shallow holes in the slabs of rock coming from the main office and then from the dunes as people could be seen running in from open desert.

Bolts also started coming from the terminal they just left but fired wildly over head and then wildly hitting office walls, rock slabs, and then into the air. Angela looked back to see Captain Jack slice the shooter's neck. As the body slumped she stabbed up under the chin into his brain.

Angela shook off the image and called out, "Cal, fighter coming in from the south and boots from the south east. Need some help, big man."

"Swinging wide for the boots. All I can do for the fighter is throw rocks."

Sounds of plasma pop and sizzle came from the arriving terminal again. The captain had jumped into a group of four mercenaries. Phase rifles making high pitched electronic feedback told Angela someone was firing point blank. The short ear piercing scream rang like an alarm clock no one could find to turn off. Angela knew the bad guys were down without seeing the bodies.

The fighter closed in just as the port defenses came alive, crossing plasma streams in front of the craft caused the fighter to break off approach to target. Suddenly Cal was the only available target for the bird. The boots had halted their charge and veered sideways toward his now retreating tugger.

Automated defenses zeroed the fighter with phase cannon's killer streams of light. The fighter dove low between outlying buildings sweeping its course away into the vast stretches of waste land. Port security staff finally in place brought sniper rifles to bear, but an armored dune skimmer swung in front of the survivors on foot, shielding them. It sped back into the dunes out of sight.

Pilots scrambling to pursuit craft heard Barney call out, "No pursuit, do not pursue, repeat, do not pursue."

Avinash took the handheld from Barney and said, "Okay Major Wisener, the action is done, perimeter is secure. You lay back."

"How bad is it, Avi?" Angela asked. Avinash gave a smile and nod while his hands twisted the improvised tourniquet.

Wing waved the medics toward them while Petey ran for electron rifles discarded by mercs at the terminal. Petey arrived to find Captain Jack searching packs and pockets in the middle of a blood orgy, Kat standing above her, rifle on hip. Petey saw four adult males and a young boy peppered with holes and blood.

"I need two rifles," he said to Kat who did not reply. Petey grabbed two and ran off wiping blood from the stocks and power packs. Wing took one of them from Petey with a questioning look back toward where Kat stood guard. Petey and Avinash stood guard over Barney's medical care givers until the stretcher took him to cover. Angela took charge of the security teams.

Chapter 24 - Aftermath

The port guard spoke to Barney sitting up in the hospital bed, "Collin Edwards was seen scampering off and several freight haulers with 'em too."

Barney said, "That means Skippy Walker is involved. Take armed constables and bring him in. No need to be gentle." Then reconsidering he said, "Reasonable force only, reasonable force!"

Turning to Angela and Cal, Barney said, "The young boy had knife wounds and an electron bolt hole. I can't prove whether she killed him or not. Goes to show, you never know about someone until fighting starts. Even the weakest coward can save your life when you have no hope, and then strand you in the desert with no shoes."

Cal was glad Petey was away helping Wing Lu load equipment on the Confederation executive transport, a sleek, shiny hulled, bullet of a ship, well shielded and armored, with a custom fit quantum generator.

"Angela, Cal, you better think hard about signing up with Jacquelin. I won't report the circumstances of her part in this action, but I like you too much to lose you to a combat crazy."

Angela said, "Not much choice in the short term, Barney. Also, we found evidence of ambushes the mercs set up in the dunes. This was all to draw us out."

"Experience is a good thing," Barney said as they shook hands and Barney said, "We still gotta get that brew, Cal."

"It'll b-be on me," Cal said.

"Of course!"

Chapter 25 – Hurts Your Head

Everyone's kit needed trimmed down for the smaller ship. Captain Jack kept her original crew of Kat and Jamie, plus she added the chief maintenance engineer whose term was up. Switching crews allowed him to stay in the military past his retirement date due to a critical shortage. The captain kept to quarters while Cal and Jamie carried unneeded seats off the ship. On the second trip Jamie's grip slipped. The Scythian stepped up and helped him lift and balance the weight until he got his hold again. Jamie's mouth dropped open.

"My name Aleksey. Thank you for try to defend me. You good man," Aleksey said patting Jamie on the back, and then walked back and disappeared behind the comm desk.

Jamie recovered and said to Cal, "You were play acting and you were going to shoot me?"

"L-Let that be a lesson."

"But who was in the … ?"

"Hurts your h-head doesn't it?"

Angela said to Cal as he stepped back onto the ship, "We need a hard talk with Kat and the captain before we break orbit."

Chapter 26 - Do Not Go Gentle

Orbit established in the freighter formerly owned by mercs. The executive transport parked in the hold allowed the crew to gather in the main seating area. Angela took charge, "If you haven't met them, the elderly gentleman is Pancho, our first class maintenance chief. The young man assisting him is Mahendra, he goes by Cisco. I assume you all know Aleksey."

Aleksey smiled, waved, and said, "Glad to be alive."

"The hot shot mechanic looking very stylish is Jimmy Ray Kim." Standing in the back, Jimmy Ray nodded.

"Now to the main reason we are here. Let's talk about over kill. Captain and Kat, what the hell happened in Wellington?" After a pause

Cal said, "Not a g-good time for u-u-uncomfortable silence. Start t-talking."

Kat said, "Jacquelin, you need to tell them."

Captain Jack said, "Not their business."

Angela said pointedly, "Captain, you are a warrior. You are good at hurting people, but can you distinguish friend from foe?"

Wing Lu asked, "Did she kill the boy? Did you kill the boy?"

To Angela she said, "I did what was necessary. The boy was on the ground, but moving when I first saw him. I don't know what happened to him after I jumped in."

Cal said, "So, yes to the f-first and m-maybe to the second."

"So you have this reputation." Angela said, "How exaggerated is it?"

Kat volunteered, "There was an episode with an assassin at a dinner party. All the Allied hierarchy and security know, Central Security certainly."

Captain Jack said, "I was doing my job. Some people have no appetite for violence."

Angela said, "But you obviously do." To the rest of the group Angela said, "Not great answers, but short term we can work with this."

Kat added, "There were rumors LaBura was cutting the captain loose until the assassination attempt in his office."

"Suddenly she's the perfect response," Angela said finishing the thought.

Kat said, "I think even Premier LaBura is afraid of her."

Angela said, "We have two ships available. If we are going to split up, this is the time. I vote to stay for now."

Petey said, "Fire or rain I'm in with my mates." Avinash and Wing Lu agreed.

Cal said, "C-Captain, you need to call the premier. Jamie found some t-toys in a c-code vault that will help."

Chapter 27 - Leverage

"Who is this!?" Premier Pieter LaBura demanded.

"Pieter, this is Jacquelin."

"Jack, where are you? You're supposed to be here with your prisoners."

"Sir, we had one live prisoner and a dead one. The prisoner who was alive told us he was ordered to kill you. He said there would be a red haired woman there to pay them. Does that make sense to you?"

"Ah, no it ..."

"Sir, we also learned there is another portal. We have a clue on how to find it. Do you want me to find it?" After some silence Jack asked, "Sir?"

"A moment, I'm thinking. Did you say red haired? Did he give you a name?"

Captain Jack said, "He only knew that a red haired woman would be there to pay him and the others. There were no other women in the office but me. What are your orders, sir?"

"Go, go find it, find the other portal," he said in a panic, "You have my authority. Shut this down. Do it quietly. Where is this prisoner now?"

"He was incinerated in the Achlys system."

"Good thinking. Yes, this will work. Jack, find the portal before it can be used again. What do you need from me?"

"Add your approval to my ID record, Sir. I'll contact you on this channel if I need anything else."

"Thank you, Jack. I'm sorry, I'm sorry for everything."

The channel went dead. An exhausted Jack turned to Cal, Angela, and Kat, "We have his authority."

Angela said, "His authority won't stop an electron torpedo, but it will keep us in supplies."

Cal said, "Sneaky trick m-mentioning the redhead. Aleksey never s-said that."

Jack smirked, "No sense letting him sleep soundly. Now we need to disappear."

Chapter 28 - Into the Good Night

"Every part of this ship with a sensor, panel, circuit, anything electronic has an ID tied to this ship. It will take years to change them all," Pancho said looking over Jamie's shoulder.

Jamie said, "Or it could take just a few minutes."

Captain Jack asked, "This will turn off all ID broadcasting, correct?"

Wing Lu said, "One code packet we loaded turns off the Confederation broadcasting. We needed a separate packet to override Scythian viruses. We also found a packet to change the ship's ID. We can rename it."

"Captain," Kat said, "We are coming up on the mercenaries' DS-2. We have bridge control. Lander is ready to launch." The massive deep space two freighter filled the screens.

"Am I the captain?" Jack asked. Cal saluted first followed by all present.

"Good," she said, then waving at the freighter on screen she declared, "Behold the Nyx, ship of night and darkness, born of chaos. Get over there. Open the hold. Once this ship is inside I want all Confederation logos and numbers removed."

Cal said, "The Nyx? You've b-been thinking ab-bout this for a long time."

Jack smirked at Cal, "The name I gave my cat."

Her gaze lingered a second, then the crew moved out. Angela said quietly to Cal outsides the bridge, "Step carefully there, Sergeant."

"What?"

Angela just looked at him, then walked away.

On Andromeda station a lieutenant reported to his commandant, "Sir, you wanted to know Jacquelin Jammula's movements. She launched on an executive transport on Cardea. The transport can't be located. There might be a magnetic storm, but we can see other craft in orbit there."

"How long ago did you lose contact?"

"Two hours, sir."

"She will show up again. If you don't find her by the end of your shift inform the Security representative."

Chapter 29 – Help Yourself

Forty eight hours later a tall cloaked woman walked a London street through fog and rain on city center square, home planet. Stopping in front of Barnard Anders Clothiers she removed her hood and stepped inside.

The very proper clerk said, "Good day, Ms. Jammula. I don't have any orders ready for the Premier. How can I help you?"

"Mr. Simms, I would like to order an outfit for myself."

"My apologies, Ms. Jammula, we only make garments for gentlemen. Perhaps I could recommend ..."

Ignoring him Jack said, "I'm looking for something all black, with a button over shirt, and riding pants."

A secret button under the counter was pushed. Low level operatives scrambled out back doors into the alley behind and into the arms of waiting security forces. Two higher ranked operatives exited a secret tunnel into the basement of Fox and Hound pub. Climbing the stairs, they calmly walked out near the men's loo, and sat at their waiting table. Barely seated, they were arrested by waiting detectives.

Ms. Jammula exited the shop to find the acting Allied security chief waiting for her. "We got them all, Captain. What are your orders?"

Captain Jack said, "Is the search complete?"

"Nearly so."

"Process them according to evidence at hand. The senior agents need processed as saboteurs. And as we discussed, leave my name out of your report. Good work, Chief."

Chapter 30 – Working Late

Hours later rubbish haulers worked down the alley collecting bins and returning to the truck. Behind a haberdashery shop an additional worker joined the effort and climbed into the cab of the truck next to the massive driver. The new passenger placed a hand on the dash to steady himself. The driver immediately flicked hand restraints around his wrist.

The alarmed passenger reached for a hidden interrupter, stopping only when he felt a muzzle against his temple coming from Petey outside the cab.

In the orbiting deep space freighter hold, among its many contents was a single chair dangling from a freight hook, its front legs barely off the deck swinging slowly on the long chain. The chair contained the security director of the Unity party safely strapped to the chair by the chest, waist, elbows, wrists, and ankles. The hook caused the chair to lean forward at an awkward angle.

The director stressed, "You can't trust her! She is unbalanced!"

Wing Lu nodded agreement, "Yes Barry Nero, we found out, but, as you know, an imbalance can be useful."

"If you know who I am then you know I am more valuable to you alive. She is insane! She could go off at any time!"

"I must disagree, Barry," Wing said pulling a long, thin knife. "We have found the captain very stable - until there is blood, then the crazy starts." At this point Wing Lu stepped forward with his hidden blade, and unexpectedly nicked the edge of the director's ear.

"What was that for?!"

Wing called toward the freight lift, "Tell the captain he is ready to talk."

The prisoner yelled, "I will not tell you anything until you release me!"

Boot steps sounded from the rows of ships and equipment. Wing Lu turned and said, "Barry, you are similar to a caught fish. You have a short shelf life. Once people know you are captured you are no good to them or to us. Look at your arm."

The stream of blood flowed down the crisp white shirt the security director wore, his working man disguise now removed. His eyes widened looking up from the red splashing flow to the approaching captain walking forward with a dull look and glazed eyes. Wing Lu said before walking away, "Short shelf life," and then handed Captain Jack the knife.

"You can't ... what do you want to know?!"

"Everything worth knowing," Wing said. The captain licked her lips, only steps from the chair.

"I'll talk! I'll tell you everything! Stop her!"

Cal stepped in from the side and wrapped his arms around the captain and growled, "Start talking. Mercenaries, Scythians, the portal, spies in the Allied party, everything."

The lander performed a perfect touch and go dumping the director onto asphalt and lifting off again.

"What do you think he will tell the party bosses?" Petey asked closing the lander door.

Cal said, "It better be c-convincing if he wants to s-survive."

Chapter 31 – What Just Happened?

Space Traffic Controller Station Five

"Ground Control Heathrow, this is OH-FIVE-THIRTY shift manager Tom Hobbs. A DS 2 just dropped off our screens. No quantum tunnel, no magnetic shift. We've warned ships in the vicinity and are running a background starlight search based on last trajectory. Will advise."

"Roger 0530. You lost a deep space transport? We will need to report to space port authority."

With a sigh Hobbs said, "I copy. 0530 out. "

"Heathrow clear."

Chapter 32 - Rage Against the Dying

Jamie raged, "We can't kill a thousand people even if they are mercenaries trying to kill us! We are becoming the monsters we are trying to stop!"

Preparations stopped cold. No quick answer came to Captain Jack or Angela. Both looked at Cal.

Angela said, "This is a one time chance to get clear of this threat to us and the Allied party, and they are still under contract to kill the premier."

Jamie said, "How do know that?"

"Barry told us, and he told us where and when they were returning," the Captain said.

"How do we know he told us the truth?" Jamie countered.

Angela said, "I assumed he mixed lies in with the truth. We will need to sort out which is which."

Wing said, "He knew about the mercenaries move on our Cardea location. Their return is logical."

Aleksey added, "If I am allowed to speak, I need to side with Jamie on principle - his principle, not mine. He did try to save me."

Cal started laughing and said to Jamie, "If we don't h-harm them in any way, but can take them out of action for a while does that s-satisfy your principles?"

Suspiciously, Jamie slowly answered, "Yes."

Cal said, "Captain, we n-need to reposition the N-Nyx."

On the Nyx's bridge all available crew watched the monitors or out the port windows.

The captain ordered, "Open the hatch, ready on trigger." A deep rumbling rattled the super structure. All waited, some held breath. The consequences of failure were known. The consequences of success were beyond imagining.

A faint glow appeared in front of the Nyx designating the arrival.

"Hold," the captain said, "hold ... hold ... Fire!"

The Nyx's quantum generator thrummed. A much larger murky area appeared. A T1 freighter and a troop transport appeared between the two glowing fields and in a flash disappeared. Glows from additional arriving tunnels appeared scattered across the monitors as the rest of the mercenary armada came through separate quantum tunnels.

The captain quickly ordered, "Kat, drop twenty degrees below ecliptic and tunnel out!"

The solar ecliptic pitched upward in the view and the generator thrummed again.

"Shut down the tunnel!" Captain Jack shouted as soon as they slipped through.

One smaller mercenary transport ship made it through and pieces of a second ship.

Angela and Avinash hurried to the air lock side of the hold to power up zero G star fighters and finish off the transport before it could do any significant damage.

Watching the fighters dance with the transport, Cal asked Kat, "Where did you send the m-mercenary freighter?"

The captain said, "I thought all their ships would come through together."

Kat said, "The aperture was wide open and aimed below the galactic ecliptic. I also doubled the max aperture time. I can only guarantee they are in free space, but I have no idea where they will end up. I'm checking star patterns recorded through the window ... No stars in the image, only galaxies on the other side. I'm not finding any matches in the catalog."

Cal said, "I h-hope they l-like each other."

Chapter 33 - Consequences

On a T1 freighter bridge somewhere in space the mercenary commander rushed in, "Captain, what is the alarm?"

"Another ship created a tunnel in front of us when we arrived in orbit. We were sucked in. We are now outside our galaxy. I have no idea where."

The commander barked, "Find home galaxy and we can work it out from there."

"That is the problem. We cannot find the Milky Way galaxy. None of the galaxies on our scan horizon are known."

Looking at the main screen showing billions of galaxies, the wave of consequences broke on his imagination. As the impact receded he grabbed at the only piece available. "Can we go backwards?"

The captain, also staring at the screen asked, "Which way is backwards?"

#

Chapter 34 - A Curse to Any Nation

Post your guards. Charge your weapons. Sail your ships.

Watch for enemies. Seek out advisors.

You ask me what I see. I see the premier tremble in his closet.

His hands shake. His held cup rattles and splashes.

Before the day I see his wife dressed in black but not mourning.

Your guards flee, and your advisors fear for themselves.

Your fear comes out of darkness unseen.

The sword of vengeance strikes surely, accurately.

Prepare your house. Appoint your successor.

No one can deliver you from the darkness you dread.

"Where did this come from?" Captain Jack asked.

Kat said, "That's why they call it a pirate glittercast. It comes from everywhere on every band, every channel. No one knows how he does it."

The intercom lit up, "C-Captain, did you see this?"

"I saw it, Cal. Everyone saw it." Switching modes the captain announced, "We're entering the system. We will be docking at Pelenor Station tomorrow. All zero craft need buttoned up for test flights while we're in port. G fighters we'll test later, on a more remote planet. Final shopping lists from maintenance and mechs need uploaded. Angela, to the bridge, please."

Kat said, "Captain, Pelenor is denying our docking request."

"Tell them to check again. We have senior executive clearance."

Kat said, "Apparently our clearance has been revoked."

Angela walked in saying, "That didn't last long."

Jack pursed her lips then said, "Kat, open up the executive channel, on speaker."

The connection completed and the voice of premier LaBura said, "Jack, I hope you are not inconvenienced too much. I didn't have a choice."

"Pieter, I've got a crew that needs to eat. We've scavenged a ship needing repairs. What are we supposed to do?"

Kat pointed to the main comm screen now showing an incoming Confederation communique.

"Jack, um, we need you to redirect to Andromeda galaxy. This prophet is getting people worked up and Unity party is threatening to call for a new government. Treaty and Dissent parties are wavering. Our whole dream could come apart."

The captain said, "You used to love the prophet. Why are you so nervous, and what are you asking me to do?"

The premier neglected to mention his repeating night terror of the prophet as a dark hooded specter with sunken eyes carrying chains and sword walking toward him through walls and doors as he fled.

Chapter 35 – Crew Time

At the mid ship day meal Jack read the communique to the crew. "Commander Jacquelin Jammula please proceed to Andromeda galaxy …"

"Blah, blah, Okay, here it is"

"Stop pirate communications originating from galactic object Swift J-0042.

Apprehend person or persons communicating as the prophet.

Destroy all communication equipment ..."

"And here is the extortion."

"... resupply will be available after successful completion of the mission."

"So," she continued, "We need to get there and get this done quickly before we starve."

Cal said, "This is how they intend to keep a l-leash on us."

Angela said, "I thought the prophet was dead. He hasn't sent a message in ten years."

"Why hasn't he been shut down?" Petey asked, "He's somewhere close to Andromeda station. Isn't he? And he didn't mention the black sword."

Avi said, "Yes, he always had a sword in there somewhere. I'll bet it's cool."

Wing Lu said, "He or she is in a pulsar system. No one wants to get close enough to find out. "

"Pulsars are based on neutron stars. How can you have any kind of system?" Jamie asked.

Jimmy Ray combed his black hair back and said, "The pulsar in Andromeda is a binary, two stars. Calus streams x-rays. Chimera, the other star, has two planets."

Several people looked at Jimmy who responded, "What? It's on the net. You can read about it yourselves. I wouldn't mind getting my hands on this sword."

Angela said, "Apparently, the search for the other portal is on hold. Aleksey, you are off the hook for now."

"Good! If Scythia learn I am alive, bad for family. Besides, I don't know where entrance. I was programmer sent to prison for knife fight. They take me out to fight with knife. Tell me nothing."

The maintenance chief, Pancho, said, "X-ray streams from a pulsar will tear through any ship or even a planet. We'll need to know the pulsar's spin pattern and rotational speed before we tunnel anywhere close to Andromeda."

Angela said, "We need to stop free access to the galley. No rationing yet."

Jimmy Ray said, "Of all the equipment we scavenged, only one lander is operational. One zero craft is safe enough to fly. We were lucky to get Avinash back after the tangle with the mercenaries."

"We have twelve zero fighters!" Captain Jack said.

"You can launch in some," Jimmy Ray said, "But getting you back in one piece is the trick. I had to cannibalize a few."

"I'm calling dibs on any swords," Wing Lu said.

Chapter 36 - Gravity Sucks

"Two planets and one moon orbit Chimera," Angela said pointing to the monitor. "The moon is a captured rock. No chance of life there. It orbits the planet Kagera, our best chance for finding a prophet in this system. Dense nitrogen, oxygen based troposphere could protect life from the two stars. The gravity is a problem. Solid iron core puts Kagera at 1.2 G, but we are detecting fluctuations."

Aleksey said, "This no good. Gravity from planet mass. You say mass come and go on big scale? Big portal maybe?"

"Maintaining a stable orbit will be a full time job," Kat said.

Captain Jack said, "If you haven't seen Chimera filtered on monitors you will want to take a look. The pulsar is pulling out a river of fire from Chimera's magnetic pole."

Wing Lu said, "This could be one of our stranger deployments if gravity is changing. We'll need pressure suits to assure blood flow and prevent nausea."

"V-Very important we don't get into punching m-matches with any inhabitants," Cal said. "Their d-denser bone structure can do some real damage. Also, interrupters don't work on them either."

Captain Jack said, "We'll be able to scan for human activity and antenna arrays as soon as we are in orbit. Jimmy Ray, will the lander handle the gravity?"

"Stress wise definitely. Cisco and I can add an additional fuel cell for extra lift."

Jack said, "Let me know when the lander is ready. Cal, have the landing party equipped and ready as soon as we complete our first orbit. The clock is humming."

Chapter 37 - Kagera

Jack, Cal, Wing Lu, and Petey stepped off the lander into the dense fog of Kagera's troposphere. The weight of air pushing down on them was felt immediately. goggles with built in comm and control panels allowed them some visibility beyond eye sight with infrared and magnetic assistance.

Cal said, "C1, r-roadway is this way."

Jack said, "Cal, drop the comm designation. Scythian wars are history, and I struggle to keep them straight."

"Sure Cap. Landing site is marked. Low comm 206 everyone. If anyone starts to feel dizzy adjust your nose tube mixture. Petey, take the lead. Wing, trail. Let's move. Buildings are half a click north."

"Why is it always me on point?"

Cal smirked, "Cause you're still the luckiest bastard I ever met."

Petey gave Cal the stink eye and led out, walking upright, electron rifle pointed down. Along the wide path through stunted trees and dense brush of muted colors. Water pooled on the trail and in the brush at every depression.

"When do we get to the road?" Petey asked over the comm channel.

"I believe this trail is the road," Cal replied.

The group walked single file up to a group of low buildings on either side of the trail. Infrared showed a short human ahead walking toward them carrying a large bundle in two arms. A short muscular man carrying an armful of dirty cloth appeared through the mist and walked past Petey's leveled rifle. He made no sound, and walked past the group without any interaction or recognition. Two other humans were detected walking across the trail and up some steps into the same building the first man had exited.

When an additional human was detected approaching the same building Cal said, "Cap, I think we are approaching a market or a pub. Might be a good place to start."

Chapter 38 – New in Town?

"Weapons outside!" A gruff voice growled as the four ducked through the low opening, pulling their goggles off.

"Petey, outside with the rifles," Jack ordered.

"Aww, I want a brew," Petey complained.

Cal frowned at Petey and watched him exit. Cal said, "No brew on duty, Petey. You know that," only to turn around to find Wing Lu holding a frothy mug and the bartender admiring a newly acquired knife.

Wing said, "What? We're here to get information. You know how pubs work. You get a drink and start talking."

Jack shrugged, "I don't have any better plan."

The dozen short men and women sitting at tables around the room stared at them threateningly. Wing lifted his mug in a salute and took a sip. His severe grimace brought derisive laughter from all.

Wing winced and said, "It tastes like alcoholic mud." He then pulled a flask out and poured a shot into the brew. He took another sip and nodded approvingly.

The bartender asked, "What you have, eh?"

Cal and Jack took seats as Wing handed the silver flask to the bartender. His suspicious sniff turned into a wide grin. Wing Lu made a drink motion with his empty hand. The tender sipped followed by raised eyebrows.

"I trade for more. You have more?"

Captain Jack asked, "Wing Lu, what do you have in there?"

"Samogon."

The captain switched comm modes and asked, "Kat, find out how much samogon Aleksey has."

Waiting for Kat's reply Jack heard a ringing in her ears. Wing's knees buckled and he steadied himself while the building creaked around them. Jack felt woozy as the room seemed to move.

"Gravity shift," Cal said grabbing the table edges to steady himself.

The inhabitants all stood and rushed to the bar. The tender refilled each mug pushed towards him as coins were thrown onto the bar.

Wing Lu's eyes swung around the ceiling as he explained, "Oh, the gravity, wow! My compass is all wobbly."

Cal stood and slid a chair over pulling Wing into it. The other customers were likewise enjoying the cheap drunk effect extra gravity provided. The experienced tender had both hands on the bar.

"Captain," Kat replied, "We are powering the ship to keep from loosing altitude. We're jumping to a higher orbit."

"Tell Jamie to drop a comm relay satellite and send me a ping every ten minutes."

Kat then said, "Aleksey has three full liters of samogon and a half liter. He says he's got a fresh mash he's just starting to heat."

Jack was interrupted by the bartender, "I trade for more drink."

Cal said, "We can only trade with the prophet."

A confused look made Jack explain, "We trade with the one who sends messages to everyone," here Jack pointed with an extended arm drawing a line across the sky.

"He no drink," the bartender said as Petey ran in saying, "Captain, we're surrounded!"

Before Cal could ask about the rifles two thick swarthy fighters stepped inside with long bladed weapons threateningly pointed across the room at hip level. The natives, wide eyed, dared not move. Captain and Cal remained seated, concealed hands on interrupters. A third taller figure stepped inside. He pointed at Jack and ordered, "Dark angel, you come."

Cal stood shielding Jack from the door giving her a chance to draw and fire, but the leader shrugged and said, "Dark angel may bring her friends if they can walk." Then he turned and walked out.

The two holding weapons remained covering the room. Wing Lu's head tilted back and forth as Cal lifted him to his feet and half supported, half drug him past the armed guards and followed Petey whining to Captain Jack, "I couldn't stay for a brew and Wing got his self fully pissed in ten minutes." The captain ignored him as she calculated the number of adversaries. Petey was right. There were at least forty armed warriors forming an escort, or guard around them, moving them away from the settlement, and away from the lander.

Chapter 39 - The Prophet

The small army led through villages of low stone homes while children, wives, parents called out to family members escorting the outlanders without slowing the column of walkers. No fear or anger were seen on villagers faces, just an acceptance of status quo.

The road or trail descended into a canyon through guarded gates of smooth stonework inserted into towering walls . The captain glanced at Cal every time they passed another fortified position and still the canyon led lower. At one point the canyon narrowed into a tight gorge where they walked in single file. A strong wind followed them lower into the darkening defile blowing forcefully at their backs.

A small widening in the track was caused by another trail coming toward them. Jack could see the approaching trail led upward again but strong hands pulled them sideways into a narrow cave opening while the main body of warriors continued past the cave. Strangely the wind rushed into the underground behind them causing Cal to lean back against the air flow push.

In a larger cave the crew were guided aside from the main trail and out of the wind blast. The larger fighter, Jack assumed was the leader, waited for them. No words were spoken. The leader held up his hand to stop their forward progress.

Suddenly the wind stopped. Before Jack could form the question in her mind the wind started again, then stopped. The process continued with uneven pauses in the wind. As her eyes accustomed to the torch light she heard and then saw the cause of the wind stopping. A gnarled old man lifted and dropped a heavy wooden frame covered in some heavy material. As the frame lifted wind poured through into blackness beyond. When he dropped the frame the wind lost it's exit and paused.

More torches were brought forward and the leader demanded of the old man, "We are here. Show me!"

The old man left the frame closed and approached. He held out his hand to Captain Jack and said, "Well hey there, I'm Henry Addison. I'm shore glad to see you folks." He shook each hand in turn except for Wing Lu, who had sat on the ground holding his head.

Jack asked, "Are you the prophet?"

"A prophet? Well, never been called that before. I'm mostly a prisoner of these messages. Speaking of which, do you have the message that brought you here? Ol' Toogo here needs to see it."

Jack pulled out her handheld, found the message and showed it to Henry and then Toogo the leader. Toogo drew a rolled up hide and opened it in the torch light. Toogo compared the hide to the back lit screen on the handheld, looking back and forth, his finger pointing to the progress he made on the hide. Jack scrolled the screen up to show the last lines.

Toogo's gaping mouth and disbelieving look staring down at the hide caused Henry to shout and dance about the cave, "I did it! I did it! I can leave! I did it!"

Toogo's slumped shoulders and stare at the closed frame sucking in minimal airflow around the edges brought Henry over to say, "Toogo, you knew this would happen someday. The shining man will tell you what to do."

Toogo dropped the hide with the message and walked out of the cave.

Henry said, "Okay, let me prop the door open and then we can go now."

"Go where?" Jack asked.

"To home planet, of course. You were sent to stop the messages. You can't destroy the opening so just take me with you. I need to meet the premier, but we need to hurry. Your craft isn't in Toogo's territory. The other warlord will probably capture it. We need to go."

Walking out of the cave against the wind flow into the gorge and up into the canyon, all along the cliffs sounds of celebration, shouting and singing preceded them. Explanations had to wait as the old man nimbly led them up the trail taking a route he knew well. Coming to the fog filled flat country the trail passed villages also celebrating. Wing Lu walked on his own strength and balance, but head hung low. Cal stayed close.

Henry broke into a slow jog. Jack striding next to him asked, "Why are they celebrating?"

Henry said, "Toogo was not a kind leader. The door was under his control as long as I was here. The door is big part of their religion. Now they are free to find another leader."

Cal asked, "What is the door?"

"I thought you knew. It's a dimensional door. This planet has many. Some flow in, some out."

Jack asked, "And your door flows out? Out to where?"

Henry pointed to the river of light swirling off of the star Chimera, and flowing across the sky. He said, "Most out doors go into the star. They affect the flow going into the pulsar."

Questioning looks from Jack and Cal caused Henry to say, "Oh sure, that's how the messaging system works. Opening and closing the door is like tapping on a table. Took a while to get the timing right. I tap the message slowly and the pulsar speeds up the signal to every possible frequency. Your radios are programmed to read the binary code."

"How did you figure this out?" Cal said.

"Oh not me. Like I said, this has been part of this peoples religion. I just tweaked their technology. I was a comm engineer from Andromeda, the Delta Station. I added the standard message header before each transmission. Problem is the angle of Chimera to the pulsar changes and the river doesn't always flow right."

"So where did you get the message content?" Jack asked.

"From God, of course."

Cal said, "Whose god?"

Henry smiled, "From my God. Well, he is now. They call him the shining man. He appears in the door sometimes, but I've had dreams too. He must have talked to the priests at some point. Toogo is a military leader, but the priests said he would be in charge until my message came back. Your hand held radio matched the words I wrote down from what the shining man told me."

Jack said, "And we are the first ship to bring your message back?"

Henry sighed and said, "No, you are number five. One crew started shooting as soon as they got here. Toogo killed them. Ten years ago a crew came but Toogo was too strong in his position. They never got to show the message. One of the early messages had a typo in the stream I sent out."

A raised eyebrow from Cal made Henry defend, "Hey, you try lifting that door in the dark and keep track of the binary code for a single word! The message you brought took three days with no sleep. It was brutal, and I had to send it over and over until Chimera and the pulsar got their angles together."

Petey asked, "How long have you been doing this?"

"Not sure how this translates to home planet, but we came here 43 annual cycles ago looking for treasure, mostly the black sword. I was the only one they kept alive."

Jack said, "If I take you back to home planet they will kill you."

"Naw, they're going to toss me in prison. Decent food, proper air flow, I can sleep when I want. It'll be a picnic compared to this place. Besides, prison will be the safest place to be when the shit starts flying."

"What shit?" Jack asked.

Henry stopped short, "You. You are the darkness the premier dreads, and quite a lovely darkness if you don't mind my saying."

Jack was stunned. Henry continued, "Your black sword of vengeance is waiting near the ship. We need to hurry."

Petey saw a weak smile from Wing.

The group put their goggles on and continued trotting the trail.

Chapter 40 – No Good Options

"Captain," Angela called, "After we lost comm with you I launched. I'm in low pattern over head."

Jack said, "We're headed to the lander with the prophet. He's skinny, probably less than 80 kilos. Run the numbers to make sure we can reach escape velocity. Also expecting an unfriendly welcome at the lander."

"Scan shows over two hundred moving toward the lander." Switching to ship comm, Angela called to the DS3, "Jamie, add eighty kilos to lander's load. What's the trajectory of escape?"

The crew heard Jamie say, "Low angle, Cap. Sending numbers to the lander. Looks like gravity is lessening. You can make it, but no room for maneuvers."

Fast trotting next to Henry, Captain Jack said, "Angela, can you delay the approaching force?"

Henry spoke up, "Don't fire at them! It'll just piss 'em off and we'll never get out of here!"

"No firing, Angela," Jack said. Then to Henry she said, "What can they do?"

"They can throw up a rain of gravel that falls like bullets. No survivors. And their heavy gravity iron knives to cut through any armor."

"What do you suggest? And I'm assuming you want to leave the planet."

Henry thought, then said, "Yeah, we'll do that."

"Do what?"

Cal said, "We can't shoot 'em. We can't hit 'em and they have the heavy knives."

Henry said, "We'll throw them a party! What do you have?"

Wing Lu lifted his haggard face and gasped out between strides, "We have samogon."

Henry gleefully said, "They'll have to capture us! Where is the, what he said?"

Jack said, "Angela, we need as much samogon as you can drop to us. How long ..."

"I have it with me, Cap, ready to drop."

"Don't bring it yet," Henry said, "We need to get to the lander."

The magnetic outline of the lander appeared through the fog as well as brightly glowing weapons of the approaching group of warriors rushing up out of the low brush brandishing any number of iron weapons.

Henry hurried forward yelling, "We need to leave on this ship." He repeated the message in the local language.

The leader and Henry argued loudly back and forth. Finally Henry turned and said, "Good news, they are taking us prisoners until we can pay the samogum-thing ransom."

Cal said, "You never asked what samogon is."

Henry raised an disbelieving eyebrow, then pointed to Wing and said, "Your friend has an hangover heavier than a neutron star. I can guess what samo-stuff is."

"Oh."

"Leave your weapons here," Henry continued, "They won't do any good, anyway."

Toogo's guards dressed individually but kept military order. These surly fighters had none of it. As the group moved their prisoners further south Cal worked over to Henry and asked what kind of group captured them.

"Toogo was like a general, maybe warlord. Still he answered to the priests. Kragger is more like a gangster, very cruel, very sadistic."

Captain Jack hissed, "Why didn't you tell us!? We could have ..."

"You could have done what?" Henry answered, "I want off this rock! This is the way off! Let it happen!"

Chapter 41 – The Black Sword

Kragger's personal foul aroma was enhanced by the blank stares and open mouths of the heads stuck on posts around his seat at the large stone table. He ate from a pile of meat inside the heavy wooden framed building. Two other large men sat eating with him and a group of armed men and women around them burned stares into the bound group in front of them. Henry spoke carefully so he did not upset the blades held at his throat.

Captain Jack said, "Tell him to take us back to the lander and we will give him one bottle of samogon when we are taking off."

Henry translated and said back to Jack, "Kragger says you bring all the drink here, now or your heads will join his table decorations."

After several exchanges Kragger conceded nothing, placing his long black blade on the table to drive home his demand. Negotiations broke off when one of the blade holders struck Henry's face crushing him to the ground. Instead of collapsing his skull Henry shook off the pain. From the floor he said, "Mum always said I was her densest child. Forty years on this planet, now I really am. I think we'll let him win this round. Give him the drink."

"Then we're dead," Jack said.

"I have an appointment with prison, and we can't push this negotiation further, so let this play out."

Jack touched her ear and said, "Angela, do you see us?"

"Right over you, Cap. Wooden building, lots of bad guys all around."

"Yes, drop the samogon outside."

"All three bottles?"

"All three."

"Three bottles away. I need to refuel, Cap. I'll call when I'm back."

The five visitors were pushed to a back wall under guard as the bottles were mixed into mugs with the local drink. The guards shouted and were swapped out with other revelers who already had a mug. The effect was praised by all as the volume of laughter and shouting brought more and more people into the building. The celebration continued with some brutal arguments leading to more hilarity and deadly fights. The noise rose higher and higher flowing outside to the grounds and other buildings. Fighters suddenly realized the tall exotic woman in the building was unguarded and started fighting their way toward her. Cal stepped in front of her, and then heard ringing in his ears. The additional weight to the alcohol changed the room into a vomitorium.

Henry said, "Follow me," as he stepped away from the swooning guards not to the door, but the toward the main table. Stepping onto a seat he reached across and grabbed Kragger's black sword and turned toward the exit. Kragger lifted his head yelling and Henry swung back around slicing Kragger's head off clean. Even in the fog of delirium shock registered around the room. Cal was stunned.

Henry quickly stepped down saying tersely, "We should leave now."

The crew followed Henry, who stopped only briefly to slice off one hand. He explained over his shoulder, "That was the man who hit me."

"Angela, where are you?" The captain called.

"Opening the outer seal now. What's your status?"

"Heading back to the lander. Need specific directions."

Angela fired the engines hovering toward the blue orb dangling in black space. "Dropping into atmo. Scanning will take a minute. Gravity is peaking. Lander won't be able to lift off until it decreases."

Henry handed the sword to Cal, "Carry this for a few minutes."

Cal almost dropped the sword. Shocked at the weight Cal cradled it across his chest, both arms bearing the burden.

"Head thirty degrees left." Angela corrected, "Turn left on the trail one click ahead. Two more clicks to the lander. Uh oh, there's another force coming from the north, twenty or more. Might be some old friends. They're coming down the trail you were on earlier."

Cal said, "Henry, people are coming from your village. What should we expect?"

"Toogo is coming!" Henry said, "I need to talk to him. This is perfect!"

Chapter 42 – Leaving it Tidy

Toogo was waiting at the lander when they got there and Toogo charged as soon as he saw them. Henry stepped forward shouting, "Kragger is dead."

"You lie!" Toogo said stopping a spear's length from Henry.

Henry pointed to Cal holding the black sword.

"Toogo, we have the black sword. If you want to lead an army Kragger's lieutenants will all be killing each other for his seat as soon as they can stand. The faster you get there the easier it will be."

After a pause Toogo said, "Give me the black sword!"

"No," Henry stated, "I need it and you don't. Settle with the lieutenants and everyone will follow you. Be kind to the people and you will lead for a long time."

Without further discussion Toogo led his troop south out of the clearing.

"Can we board the ship now?" Jack asked Henry.

Henry growled, "Why are you asking? Open the door. Let's get out off this rock!"

Chapter 43 - Andromeda Alpha Station

"Look m-miserable," Cal said.

Henry's face went slack.

"Commander, you can see the prisoner is in our custody. There are no more binary messages streaming from Chimera to the pulsar. What more evidence do you need?"

"Very good, Captain Jammula. We will send over supplies on the next shuttle run. The parts will take longer. Not all of them are on Alpha. I'll send runners. While you wait, may I offer you the hospitality of our finest accommodations and dining? Rumors of your travels have many of us intrigued. We have no food shortages out here and would love to have you regale us with your first hand accounts."

"That is a gracious offer, Commander, but I am exhausted and most of the stories are classified."

"If you change your mind, I can offer marinated cybrian roast. We are famous for it."

"Thank you again, but right now I only want a shower and rack time. Nyx, signing off."

The line went dead. The camera in the brig switched off. Cal stepped forward with keys to the manacles. He said, "Y-You're a good sport, Henry. Hope th-that's our last charade."

"Not likely, Cal. It's still a long road to prison."

"Sure you won't let us drop you off somewhere safer?"

Henry smiled taking the clean clothes from Cal, "You just get me there. It will all work out, but not well for many."

Cal squinted at the thin old man and said, "You been talking to that shiny guy."

Henry whispered, "You'll also find security has changed since you left home planet, tighter in some places, looser in others, so go careful." Then Henry called to Petey and Wing Lu, "I'll wager every kid you two grew up with would be shocked you have touched the real black sword. Well now, quit your bothering and close the floor hatch. We don't want any bad guys finding that thing yet."

Chapter 44 – Rough Landing

"No, no portals. I want to travel like a normal person. No gadgets, no gizmos. Just normal like. Quantum is fine, just no trap doors."

Captain Jack spoke to the air, "That might be difficult, Mr. Addison. My orders are to stop you. They said nothing about capturing you. I'm sure my orders will change when they hear you are in custody."

The group gathered around Henry in the hold stopped talking while Henry answered the Captain's comm from the bridge,

"Ah, they didn't come right out and say kill me. Playing it safe! Very smart, but it won't help 'em. I'm gonna land right on their doorstep without so much as a please and thank you. Then they'll have to deal with me themselves. Won't be so easy."

"Captain," Kat said, "they're repeating your orders on all channels now, asking you to acknowledge."

"Okay Henry," the captain sighed, "we will get you back to home planet somehow."

"Oh, I'm not going back. This'll be my first trip. I'm an outlander born and raised. My grand parents settled Mistral in the Zagros system."

"Henry, you were explaining," Jamie said.

Henry looked up to the upper deck and said, "Captain, we gotta get closer, at least inside Jupiter."

Then to Jamie, Henry said, "You think of time and space as solid blankets with a few holes. They're more like nets filled with gaps, it's all gaps, but we're anchored onto a few strings. On Kagera I saw whole mountains built from the output of a single dimensional door, and the majority of the volume coming out was gas. Rocks were a byproduct. S'what makes the gravity bounce around."

Food was served on make shift tables in the main hold, far from the galley. Henry preferred the wide open feel. Pancho and Cisco sat in the open cargo door of a lander, Jimmy Ray perched on the boarding ramp for the shiny executive transport. Others sat on crates or maintenance stools.

Cal asked, "Why are there so many portals on Kagera?"

"Planet's riddled with agridot. Stuff's stable enough until until it's disturbed. Then look out. No telling where you or just part of you will end up."

Wing said, "As a child I was told stories of a magical black sword. Does the black sword have powers?"

Henry said, "Ya know what magic is. It's science ya don't understand yet, or simple deception. Either way, these stories get told and believed, especially by people greedy for the magic."

Captain Jack exited the freight elevator saying, "I found a military convoy going our way, The commander is a friend of my father. We can hitch a ride to Mars orbit. After that, we're on our own. We're tunneling to meet them as soon as we are secured.

"Henry, I apologize," Jack continued, "but you will need to be in chains when their pilot boards. I can leave a key, just make sure you look sad when the camera comes on."

"I'm so excited to be this close, looking sad'll be a chore."

Jack said, "Do your best. Wing Lu, meet the pilot, escort him to the bridge. Aleksey, please be scarce, that means hide ... someplace comfortable."

"I know scarce. Yes, captain boss."

"And make sure the samogon is out of sight and the smell is evacuated before you hide. Jimmy Ray, is this lander operational? Then button it up for the jump."

Pointing at Angela Jack ordered, "You and Avinash line up the transport and lander for deployment."

Chapter 45 – Military Escort

As soon as the quantum alarms ceased the air lock operation alarms rang out. The pilot exited his lander as the inner doors sealed. Wing Lu entered the sealed door and was shot twice in the chest, wide burn holes ended his story. Pancho watched from his office window above as commandos exited the lander racing through the door and up the stairs. Pancho rang the all-stations alarm as his last act.

Angela looked up at the sound of running boots on the stairs. She grabbed Cal's arm as he ran for the elevator. "It's too late, Cal. The ship is lost. Get in the Transport. I'm going to blast our way out of here."

Her plans changed as electron bolts forced them to take cover in the lander. Aleksey was hiding in the back and demanded. "Why are we in shit?"

Ignoring him Angela shouted into the comm, "Who is in the transport?"

Avinash said, "I'm still in here. What is happening?"

"We've been boarded," Angela said. Then turning to Cal she ordered, "Open the side door. Petey is out there!"

Angela continued, "Avi, pivot your guns on the inner doors! Wait, open the transport freight hatch. Jamie and Cisco are trying to get in!"

Cal countermanded the order, "Angela, we're in the middle of a convoy. They'll burn us as we exit. Power up the quantum generator!"

As Jamie, Jimmy Ray, and Cisco scrambled aboard the transport Avi said, "But that will compromise the ship!"

"Just do it!" Cal ordered.

Both craft powered up causing the commandos to redirect fire to engine exhausts, the only way to cripple zero vehicles with electron bolts.

The sound of the quantum cavity opening was masked by engines and the fire fight raging. The far side of the hold blurred and and the vacuum of space sucked out anything not bolted down, equipment, personnel, air, and then it was over. The Nyx and convoy were gone. Only free floating people, parts, and the two small craft remained.

Angela called out, "Avi, don't leave us behind, but we need to tunnel again quickly in case the bodies out there have tracers on them."

The two craft slipped out of the debris field and disappeared together.

Chapter 46 - Message Received

Jacquelin's eyes watered involuntarily from the fist to her nose. Two spec soldiers held her secure while the lieutenant struck her again. Others applied first aid to their comrades unfortunate enough to be standing in the door when the emergency hull breach shields deployed All critical openings slammed shut severing a hand and partial leg.

Still, they fared better than Kat, blown sideways out of her seat from multiple weapons, her vacant eyes staring.

"Lieutenant, two captured, three down, seven escaped."

"How did they escape?" The officer demanded.

"They powered up a quantum tunnel in the hold breaching the hull. The tunnel closed, and the ship is sound. Four commandos were ejected with the escape vehicles. Zero fighters were sent to intercept."

"They'll be gone. Open the airlock for the commander's transport."

"Aye, Sir."

"Ms. Jammula, you have disobeyed direct orders. You are stripped of rank, privilege, and protection. You are at Commander Hernandez' mercy. Answer his questions quickly, completely and you might live."

Jack's head hung low, dripping blood and mucous, making no sound, but looking sideways at Kat.

A muscular mercenary strode through as the door slid open.

"I've been chasing this bitch forever. Now she's gone and killed our whole command. Some pay back is due I'd say!"

He grabbed her tunic and jerked side ways, but the combat garment did not yield. He ripped at it again twisting her sideways out of the grasp of the guard on her left. Her legs tensed and a stiffened foot sent a crushing blow into the mercenaries testicles sending him to the floor, writhing in pain and nausea.

The guards reacquired their hold on her as Commander Hernandez entered. The Commander looked down and stepped around the pale, bug eyed mercenary and said, "You do your father proud. Jacquelin."

Jack's head tilted up defiantly still dripping red colored mucous.

"Your father is in La Jornada Prison. What happens to you and him will be determined by how much you are willing to cooperate. Your brother's life will also hang in the balance when we find him. And we will find him."

Jack said nothing.

Hernandez turned to the Lieutenant and said, "First things first. Find the Prophet and kill him."

Eyes turned to the monitor covering the brig. The prophet's cell was empty, manacles laying open.

"Find him!"

Chapter 47 – Not Again!

The search was shortened by a call from the convoy, "Commander, fleet command says the Prophet is transmitting open broad band from your location."

The electronic utility closet was opened.

"What did you say?" Commander Hernandez demanded.

"That was a hell of a lot easier than lifting that damned wooden frame, a lot quicker too. Don't get your knickers in a twist. It's all recorded. You won't miss anything. You will, however, need to check in with your bosses before you shoot me or anything."

Every hand held in the communications bay and around the ship began chirping. The Commander answered his.

"Commander Hernandez, this is fleet command. Stand down. Do not harm the person calling themselves the Prophet. This is General Turskey. I repeat, do not harm the Prophet!"

"New orders," the Commander declared, "We are taking the Prophet and Ms. Jammula into custody. The Prophet will be delivered unharmed to civil authorities for prosecution. Lieutenant, you will take charge of the prisoners and be responsible for their health and appearance."

The Lieutenant blanched, knowing Jack's eyes were already blackening from the broken nose, "But sir, I was following orders, and ..."

Hernandez held up a hand, "See that nothing else happens to her. Not one mercenary is to touch or even talk to her. Have a female officer get her cleaned up, clean clothes, but no uniforms."

"General," a soldier burst in, "We found it!"

Two other men struggled forward with a long, thin burden wrapped in canvas. The Commander lifted the top layer to reveal a black, double edged, straight sword with open handle and straight hilt.

"Is this your's?" Hernandez asked Henry.

Henry said, "It goes with the Captain."

"This is a jian blade from the Tsang Dominion. Very ancient."

"Don't know. It came from a gangster on Kagera."

"It's been modified. Why is it so heavy?"

"Don't know too much about sword making."

The General said, "Load this on the transport. Make sure Ms. Jammula does not get near it."

Chapter 48 – Unexpected Developments

The emergency override protocol had preceded the Prophet's message forcing all media and all military to transmit the words of revolution. Each center of government had aides calling leaders to windows and monitors to witness people running to congregate. Within hours tents started appearing. Sanitation workers, following protocols, set up temporary facilities. Orders recalling support for the people roused savage responses from the growing masses.

Unpaid local military and police joined the throngs, organizing and strengthening the determination of crowds to find hope despite the rampant corruption denying them justice, livelihood, and food.

The darkness is coming. You cannot hold it back.

Draw your weapons, eliminate your enemies.

Each body you leave bleeding turns into one of your friends, your family.

You are already caught in your own trap but can't see the teeth closing.

Your name becomes the synonym for panic, hysteria.

The peaceful reluctantly march to take your place.

The humble lift me up says the Lord.

They will be lifted up.

People, come to the steps of government to hear the voice of God.

They hear sound of liars and still they come for hope.

Hope will be given to them.

Dark floods rage, purging halls and offices of depravity then flow away.

Two days will be the requirement for justice.

Mercy for the merciful, peace for the peaceful in two days.

Come people, come to the center of intrigue.

Witness your deliverance.

Chapter 49 - Sliver of Hope

"You can't possibly know that!"

"Angela, Henry gets visits from this glowing guy who tells him stuff. The stuff happens. This message says Henry will get to home planet in two days."

"Cal, you like her. Any fool can see it, but you're reaching beyond hope to find her."

Petey whispered to Aleksey, "Who's Angela talking about?"

Floating in free space the two vehicles debated their choices when the Prophet's message dominated all communication channels.

Angela said, "We have no water or food. This is our moment of decision. There is no turning back from our next step. We can make the Rigel outpost or head to home planet."

Then shaking her head Angela added, "And how do we get past solar patrols? How do we get to the capitol building where you think Henry will be? And how do you know Jack will be there?"

Cal said, "We can tunnel into the shadow of Io, then find Aleksey's portal."

"Aleksey has no idea where the portal is! You've no chance of finding it."

Cal desperately scanned the interior of the lander for some glimmer."

Aleksey raised his hand, "I don't know where portal is, but maybe socks know."

Angela and Cal zeroed in on the Scythian. Petey looked back and forth not following the conversation.

"You took uniform and burned. Mother made socks for me. I hid them. Space is cold. Socks are warm."

Angela glared at him.

"I wash socks but maybe pollen still there. Tell us where I was?"

Angela, exasperated, said, "You have fifteen minutes, no more."

Cal held out his hand, "Socks Aleksey!"

The bio scanner picked up no traces of vegetable matter.

Angela nodded and spoke to the transport, "Avinash, calculate jumps to Rigel."

"Wait!" Cal said, "Aleksey, your boots!"

"But you give boots," Aleksey said.

"Yes, but your socks were in the boots before all the washing!"

Aleksey handed over his boots. Predictably, the left one offered no help, common grasses and flowers from many planets. Scanning the right boot lining showed pollen from pinot noir grapes found in many home world countries, and azoreta compacta grown only in Andean highland areas.

Angela said, "You've narrowed the possibilities to highlands in South America with vineyards. Not good enough, Cal. Three minutes to go."

"Something's blocking the micro prism. Hang on, there's a piece of shmutz in there. Gotcha!"

Cal rotated the gear to use the larger opening focusing on the thin fiber. The monitor registered tillandsia samaipatensis, found only in the region Samaipata, Bolivia.

"Are there any large cave systems in the area?" Angela asked.

"The net says no caves, but there are large stone structures nearby, a place called the Volcanoes, and a big stone called El Fuerte, meaning strong or fort."

"Let's see it."

The image on the screen stunned and converted all to Cal's side. The image of El Fuerte showed a series of ancient shallow stone doorways carved into a rounded sandstone mound, more weather worn, but identical to the temple on Onyx.

"Twenty seconds to spare, Cal. Avinash, we are heading to home planet. Can you hop us into the scan shadow of Io?"

"I am not as good as Kat, but I'll give it my best."

"Small steps, Avinash. I don't want to end up parked next to the mercenary troop transport in unmapped space."

Chapter 50 – Heading Home

Three hops later, lander in tow, Avinash glided into a parallel orbit with Charon, the perfect vantage point for solar range jumps.

Angela said, "Avinash, let the generator guide you. If you scan from this distance you'll give our position away."

Jamie said, "We got bits of a scan from a patrol ship between us and Neptune. Their next look 'round will catch us."

"You can almost see Jupiter from here, Avi," Cal said, "Don't wait about. Let's go!"

Avinash inhaled and levered open the generator. The view on the other side of the tunnel was perfectly between Jupiter and Io, the two vehicles leaned forward. The tunnel closed behind them. A quick scan of their location revealed a patrol ship immediately next to them, a mid solar guard ship, heavily armed. All held their breath. No scan was needed, proximity warnings on the patrol ship already revealed them. Zero fighters could be launched in seconds ... a minute if they were between shifts.

Five minutes later, "Maybe their door shield is ..."

The door shield came into view. It looked fine. One crewman could be seen viewing his monitor inside the airlock hold, but no challenging hail came.

Jimmy Ray let out his breath, "What are they waiting for? They have to know we're here."

"Maybe it's the Prophet?" Cal guessed, "Maybe he's causing a ruckus and no one will be looking when we land."

Angela said, "Let's not risk it. We're probably too small for them to worry about. Avinash, swing around in front of Io before we tunnel. Take us to the open between Mars and home planet. No point looking suspicious when we can't hide anyway."

The additional hop placing them in level five synchronous orbit over South America brought no challenge from Southern Port Authority.

"Okay Avinash, take us down to level two orbit over the target. The lander can manage from there. Go find a pad and get some food and rest."

Chapter 51 – Incarcerated

Jack was a pro. Small setbacks like getting her face beaten, her crew murdered in front of her, being the target for every branch of her government in concert with an enemy empire, betrayed by old friends, while her hands and feet were chained - she rejected despair. Anger was a better choice - controlled, focused, pent up potential energy. She was a pro. Soldiers guarding her could not see it. For Jack and the planet at large, small events continued to fall on the growing imbalance under weakening restraints: like an avalanche, the destruction is slow and then sudden and indiscriminate.

Helen, Pieter's wife Jack's one time friend, walked into the containment area escorted by two guards. Journalists were not allowed. Jacquelin lay on the bunk, an arm across her face revealing her chains.

"I'm sorry Jack. I tried to get you a room, but Emir Vos insists on making an example of you. Now we see who is really in control. All our work - we fooled ourselves. They wouldn't tell me the charges against you. Can you tell me?"

Jack spoke from under her arm, "The whole would take some time. The brief list starts with us stopping Vos's assassination of Pieter. The Emir also thinks I killed his son. I uncovered their use of mercenaries, and the Emir's plot with the Scythians. He may not be aware, but I also compromised his security chief."

Helen said, "Barry Nero? He's dead."

"Then he does know. Also, the Emir's daughter is sleeping with Pieter."

Helen looked down and said, "Not exactly sleeping. Yes, it's the big secret everyone knows."

Shifting her stance Helen asked, "Jack we were good friends once. Is it too late to be friends again?"

Jacquelin uncovered her face and sat up. Helen gasped.

Jack said flatly, "If you want to be my friend, Do one thing for me."

"If I can."

"Stay away from Pieter. Stay far away."

"All the parties are planning a big event tomorrow on the capital steps. Pieter and the other parties are announcing sweeping reforms. I need to be there. I'm Pieter's good will ambassador."

"Then stay close to a door."

"What's going to happen, Jack?"

"I don't know, but Henry the Prophet knew he would be on the capital steps, and he threatened Pieter with his messages. Henry seems a funny little man but he's extremely dangerous."

Chapter 52 – Samaipata

"Does anything look familiar, Aleksey?"

Cal said, "Put down over there, Angela. That will give us c-cover for the lander."

Angela barked, "Petey, sit down. You're crowding me."

"Sorry."

Feet touched down. The door opened.

Aleksey said, "I came at dark. See nothing, but smell is same."

Petey said, "I feel naked without a weapon."

"It's more than a little strange Southern Port Authority let us land without a challenge," Angela said, "Cal, lead us up the hill."

The trail led out of the clearing into steep, high jungle. The domed rock of El Fuerte was visible in the fading light past a row of low buildings. Cal raised his hand for caution when the interrupter blast hit him in the chest. Other blasts echoed in his mind as his senses failed.

The boot to his ribs brought him to consciousness. Cal became aware of shouting, then realized they were shouting at him. Angela and Petey lay next to him hands and feet tied together and laying in front of the lander. Above the shouting, hammering on the compressed fiber of the lander door filled the air. Happy shouts came from the door side and sounds of the door grinding open. Men and women, not in uniform but clearly Scythian military, combed through the equipment as it was ejected from the door.

Exuberant shouting began and Cal saw one of the Scythians holding a metallic canister and shouting. It was one Aleksey used for samogon. This meant the entire store of samogon and probably the still also were stored in the back of the lander, an additional chaotic turn Cal didn't need. He began to wonder where Aleksey was.

Chapter 53 – Another Point of View

Earlier Petey sealed the lander door and stepped ahead of Aleksey heading up the trail. Before taking one step a fragment of memory came to Aleksey of Scythian soldiers singing up ahead around a campfire as he walked uphill. This time he never started walking. The interrupter blasts hit Cal and Angela. Petey ran sideways, directly into the next round of fire. Aleksey dove behind the lander, crawling into low brush. The ambush came from the front and left side. They never saw him.

Crawling further back, he hung his head when the samogon was found. The outcome was well known for his new friends, especially Angela.

Then he heard female voices among the soldiers. Peeking out he felt sick. He had killed his sister's abusive boyfriend with a knife, and gone to prison. Now his sister, Nadia, was celebrating the samogon find with her fellow soldiers. One abusive boyfriend suddenly multiplied into twenty or more drunk, abusive confederates, including several officers.

All his sacrifice for his little sister only led to a more vile outcome for her. Remote outposts did not need alcohol for violations to happen, but samogon guaranteed it.

The canisters were carried jubilantly up to the low huts where they were housed. Nadia and the other woman soldier stayed behind to finish looking through the lander and guard the prisoners.

Eventually the other woman went inside the lander. Aleksey quietly called out, "Sladkiy gus, idi siyuda" (Sweet goose, come here).

"Aleksey? Aleksey, eto ty?" (Is that you).

Nadia walked behind the lander, interrupter leveled.

Aleksey stepped out where no portals in the lander could see him, hands raised.

(In Scythian)

"Hello sweet little goose. You are so grown up!"

They both cried in a strong hug, but then she pulled back.

"Aleksey, I was told you were dead. Did you come out one of the doors?"

"Nadia, you and your comrade are in big danger. The men, some have been here a long time. When somogon is drunk they will come for the lady prisoner and then they will come for you and your friend. I was here before. I heard talk about women in local village."

Nadia said, "There no women in village. Only few old men." Then Nadia looked disgusted and said, "They would be arrested if they did!"

Aleksey shook his head, "They will make sure you do not talk."

Nadia paused then said, "No, these good soldiers. What you are saying is not right."

Aleksey looked her in the eyes and said, "You are not the first."

"Nadia!" The other woman called out. "What are you doing over there? They just dragged the woman prisoner away. What did they say to you?"

Nadia ran to the prisoners and could see in the fading light, the woman struggling against the bonds as she was dragged up the hill. Nadia turned to the other prisoners. Their eyes wide open, but mouths were stuffed with leaves and taped over.

Aleksey came up and said, "Nadia, these my friends. I need to help them."

The other woman came around the lander, "Nadia, who is this? Who are you?"

"Katya, put gun away. This my brother Aleksey, He is brother I told you about."

"But he is not dead!"

Aleksey said, "Very long story, but these my friends. We hiding from home planet soldiers. You not supposed to be here."

Katya said, "We fight for Scythian peoples."

Nadia stepped in, "Katya, Aleksey is big hero. He fights for Scythia also, but they took woman for pleasure. They get drunk and they will come for us."

Steps coming down sounded in the growing dark. A voice called out, "Nadia, I am here to replace you. Go up for dinner."

Aleksey stepped back behind the lander.

Nadia looked past him and called back, "Fires are not lit. Where is smoke from fires? Why are you lying to me?"

Three soldiers approached the lander and prisoners.

One said, "Your turn to make food, Nadia. Come."

Katya said, "I saw no one collect firewood. How can we cook?"

The soldier grabbed Nadia's wrist as gunfire sounded from the camp, not interrupters but electron blasts. Two soldiers turned, but the one gripping Nadia's arm was focused on her. He didn't notice the shadow roll out from under the lander, grab Katya's gun and press the muzzle against the soldier's head.

"Slowly let go, or you die!"

The soldier jerked Nadia into Aleksey but the trigger was already in motion. The close blast burned into the side of his head, dropping him. The other soldiers turned to Nadia as she drew her weapon and fired.

Katya said through clenched teeth, "Nadia, what have you done?"

Nadia holstered her interrupter and said, "They are not dead. I am preserving military order."

She opened a knife and cut the bonds holding Cal and then Petey, and said, "Aleksey, tell your friends to help the woman."

Gun fire slowed but continued. Cal and Petey jumped to their feet. (In English)

Pointing to the unconscious soldiers Aleksey said, "Take interrupters and help Angela! I stay and guard my sister."

Petey said, "Right."

Running up the hill, Cal and Petey hid behind the first in a row of connected shacks and peeked out. Two bodies were visible. A single electron sounded. Cal snuck Bent over around the front, Petey followed. The first two shacks had a single door in front, while the next two were open shelters. Small, four wheeled vehicles were parked, and Cal saw three Scythians hiding behind them facing a door into the fifth shack. The smell of burnt flesh hung in the air.

Wasting no time, Cal signaled to Petey and they rushed the soldiers firing and keeping low. The three went down; Cal and Petey acquired their vantage point. Another body lay across the opening into the fifth shack, multiple burn holes visible in his torso.

Cal spoke low, "Angela, It's Cal. I'm coming in."

Petey hung back covering while Cal slunk to the door, not exposing himself to Angela's fire. Cal looked in and pulled back quickly. Angela's weapon lay across another body just inside the door.

"Angela, it's Cal," brought no response. Cal swung around the corner knocking the gun sideways. Angela had two burn holes coming out of her back. Cal rolled her over.

"Angela, got here fast as I could."

Her eyes opened, A brief grimace turned into a weak smile, "How'd I do, Cal?"

Cal looked around the shack. Another body lay against the back wall.

"You got five of 'em, Ange. Denise would be proud," Cal said. "Petey and I got three. Where's the rest?"

Angela did not answer. Her fighting was done.

Chapter 54 - Prelude to a Massacre

"We are not going to let you speak to the crowds unless you tell us what you are going to say!"

The prophet, Henry, calmly repeated for the twentieth time, "If I don't know what I'm going to say then I can't tell you." Then laying back on his cell bunk he added, "But no worries, I've got loads of time. Do you?"

"You said you needed to speak tomorrow. Don't you need to make that happen?"

Henry said, "Naw, my job's to say the words I'm told. The rest is up to the shiny guy. Let him figure it out."

Behind the darkened glass the technician told the yawning Pieter, "We just need to keep him talking. We'll control the audio and video. We'll use his own voice to adjust his words as needed."

The Premier turned to the soldiers escorting him, "Tell the Emir and members I will be a few minutes late. I want to be present when they interrogate Ms. Jammula. I will be up shortly."

One soldier saluted, pivoted, and walked out, walked straight to his command post and signaled his commander, "The Premier is coming up to see Ms. Jammula."

The commander called the cell block, "Is she presentable? The Premier wants to see her before his cabinet meeting."

"You're joking right? The Premier said no harm to her, but she looks like hell. We tried some make up but it's pasty at best."

The commander said, "It will be brief. He's in a rush. Keep the lights low and find something to shadow her face."

Pieter's new schedule coordinator lectured him, "Red Sky workers are threatening to strike if the Prophet doesn't show, and we'll lose Red Sky support. Emir Vos and the cabinet are waiting."

"This will only take a moment. She's right in here," Pieter said.

Opening the door of his private office, the Premier saw a hooded, pale specter with darkened eyes. The guards, unseen in the shadows, struggled to get her restraints unlocked. One hand unbound and the chain rattled free dangling from one hand, white eyes in sunken sockets glaring.

The sleep deprived Premier, electrified into panic, as the recurring nightmare walked into his office. He fell back knocking over a lamp leaving the specter back lit as one guard rushed forward to help in the dark. Fighting off the unexpected help with cries of "No! No!", the Premier got to the secret door behind him and closed himself in his private bedroom, locking the door.

Pouring himself a glass of scotch, he held it with two hands to steady the shaking. The door swung open again framing the ghoul. The Premier screamed and bolted to the next door on the other side. In the dim light the door he just locked unlocked on it's own. Pieter pulled the antique pistol hidden in the drawer and pointed it.

The woman opening the door calling, "Pieter, it's me," could not be heard above the terror in his mind. The explosion blew an opening through the intruder's body.

Turning on the lights, Pieter saw the blood and red hair mixed together.

Chapter 55 – Distant Sounds

Cal heard rumbling, then Petey called out, "Name yourselves!"

"Petey, it is Aleksey. Don't shoot!"

Cal crouched in the doorway, backing up Petey as Aleksey, Nadia, and Katya came into the opening calling, "The doors are opened! Where is Angela?"

Petey looked behind and saw Cal's tears and pistol pointed at Aleksey.

"Angela is gone, Aleksey," Cal said wiping tears on his sleeve, "but I need to know who's side you are on."

"Angela good woman. I see she die fighting. Very sorry," Aleksey said putting his interrupter into the holster he now wore, he raised his hands and said, "Cal, you know me. I am Scythian. My blood, my family is Scythian. I do not like officers, but I am still Scythian. You treat me like friend. We are friends. I do not lie to you. If I help you find Captain, you don't stop me."

"You're going to kill the Premier?"

Aleksey pointed to his sister, "We are going to try. Will you fight us?"

Cal stood, holstered the electron pistol he took from Angela, and said, "No, I s'pose not, but I won't help you either."

"This good," Aleksey said, "We must hurry reopen portal doors. Many soldiers already go. Leave guns. Take knives."

Chapter 56 – The Other Door

The deep darkness of a clear mountain sky at night shot through with so many stars stunned Cal, now climbing the short distance up the hill to the massive sloping stone of El Fuerte. He looked up with eyes wide. The disappointment of Katya coming up on a four wheeler, displacing the quiet and the darkness was equally profound. She hopped off and powered up a diesel generator, threw a switch and the entire red stone dome, as big as a football pitch, was painted with light.

The top of the stone had two deep grooves, a foot wide and deep, running most of the length from top to bottom. Both grooves had a smooth, white stone blocks sunk into the bottom of the long grooves. Joined across tops of the white blocks by a metal framework, pulleys connected to a thicker cable leading to the top of the stone. The whites stones, Cal could see were getting dragged up and down the grooves.

Katya hooked her machine to a cable and started pulling the two white blocks up the grooves, stone against stone, to the top. The grinding sent strange but familiar vibrations through Cal. As frantic as he felt to find Jack, the shuddering of the blocks against the red sandstone gave a peace to his mind and soul, a strange but familiar euphoria, almost like ... and the rock faded from his sight. Suddenly Cal saw children of every color on sunlit hillsides They glowed and played, laughing, singing, and calling to each other. Some looked at Cal waving and saying something he could not understand. Weeping, he wanted to go to them more than anything. One calling to him looked like his brother.

Cal reached out his hand, but Aleksey's shouting interrupted the vision, "Why you are crying? Stand inside door. The white stones will be dragged down. The vibration will open doors. Do not be afraid."

Nadia took Cal's hand and led him sobbing over to a doorway. She said something in Scythian. Cal didn't know the words, but they comforted him.

Petey asked, "Aleksey, where will the doors take us?"

Aleksey said, "Not where, but when. Makes head hurt. But, first we need agridot."

The blocks stopped at the top. Katya backed up the vehicle and switched cables. Getting back on she revered her engine yelling, "Gotov!" The four wheeler jumped forward. The vibrations pierced Caleb's brain and South America disappeared.

Petey waited for something to happen, then stepped back from his door, and saw the fracture lines running through it. He stood alone.

Chapter 57 – A Pale Rider

Emir Vos huddled with his closest deputies in a side room off the larger cabinet hall. The minister of Security spoke low, "The shooters in the upper floors will focus on Pieter and his wife. Shooters in the crowd will hit random targets as soon as Pieter goes down."

The minister of Information nodded saying, "The video edits are already created. We will intersperse with live coverage from the crowd."

Vos fumed, "I want this broadcast immediately. You must show Pieter's body."

"We already have the footage in case of any delay."

Vos stood and said, "Agree to anything Pieter requests in the Cabinet meeting.

An aide entered and whispered in Emir Vos's ear. The Emir's face paled and he dashed from the room.

Pieter's private doctor worked furiously to stop the bleeding as Emir Vos's daughter fought for breath on Pieter's bed. Medics were in route. In Pieter's outer office the security commander grabbed Jack's arm forcing her back and rushed her down the main corridor away from the scene. People gathered in the outer hall. A bell announced the arrival of an elevator car.

Jack, still in the black cape and hood, growled to the commander, "If the Emir finds out you brought me here you will die here and now."

The commander watched the elevator door start to open and he whisked Jack into the Security Chief's office, her old office. The Emir rushed past with his entourage. After he passed the commander grabbed Jack's arm again, causing the dangling chain to strike a metal chair. A fiery glance exchanged, then the blows started.

The commander was taller, heavier, but Jack was hardened, gifted, experienced, and furious. She fended off his initial attack and erupted her blinding, focused fury with lethal effect to his eyes, throat, groin, and finished off with an undefended kick to the head.

Grabbing his electronic key, Jack strode back to Pieter's office in time to see the Emir grab Pieter's pistol from a guard and fire three rounds at the fleeing Premier, leaving holes in the wall. Another guard, not quick enough was hit and fell back through the secret door revealing new carnage in the bedroom. The doctor and his patient both lay bleeding out from the Emir's shots through the wall, while Pieter escaped.

Jack moved back down the main corridor and opened a door revealing a narrow passage for moving VIPs and other clandestine visitors to his personal office. Before she stepped into the narrow hallway a guard coming out of the Premier's office shouted, "Stop!"

His raised electron blaster jerked wildly from an unseen force, and then the guard lurched sideways, blood spilling from wounds torn in his stomach and then throat. Jack knew the cause. She had no defense and little time. She noted the time on a wall clock and entered the narrow hall.

An escaping Premier dashed into the same passageway farther down, turned and saw the hooded black robed phantom rushing at him. Multiple high security doors slammed closed to stop it or slow it down to no effect. He stumbled and scrambled to the one door where he could find safety, security, solace. He dashed inside slamming the door on the specter.

Helen looked up from her desk, "What are ..."

The door burst open. The black intruder pulled back the hood.

Pieter cried out, "No, get it away!"

Helen said, "Take him. He's all yours. By the by, nice costume, Jack."

"Huh?"escaped from Pieter's open mouth.

Jack put a hard knee in Pieter's chest, "I should kill you for what you did to Kat, and the others."

Helen cried, "Kat is dead?

"If not by his order, then by his silence!"

Jack viciously head slapped Pieter and said, "Listen to me! I need Henry, the Prophet, and the black sword here now!"

"Uh, I, he, he's in the cells."

Jack swung another slap Pieter blocked. Jack grabbed two fingers and snapped them back making a loud crunch.

"Ahhh!"

"Get him here now! Where is the sword?"

"It's in, in the side cabinet in my office."

"Give me your handheld!" Jack demanded.

Jack took it and punched in a well known number and shoved the device to Pieter's ear, "Tell them you want the Prophet up to Helen's office now!"

The jailer agreed.

Jack turned to Helen, "I need a bed sheet and black spray paint from the janitor's closet."

Helen returned and Jack uncapped a spray can and said, "Helen, I need to mark your walls." Jack removed a painting from the wall and froze. Carved into the wall behind the painting she found a series of letters and numbers:

C1

~~P1~~ S1

~~WS1~~ GS1

Samogon +1

SAPA Wide Open

Pieter's light fixture

If we escape - ILY

After a stunned moment Helen said, "I understand the last line, but what does the rest mean?"

"Cal?" whispered Jack, and she added to Helen, "It means I lost two more ... friends." Jack choked up and said, "I never imagined. Cal?"

Then straitening up she announced, "I don't have time. There's no time. Helen, I need a strange favor."

"Anything."

Jack spread out the sheet and sprayed while saying, "I need you to hold up this sign in Pieter's office facing the door to the outer hallway, only for a few seconds."

A quizzical look from Helen made Jack say, "Don't worry, you'll make it back fine, and you won't be followed."

"How can you know that?"

"Because we're having this conversation. Trust me on this. Also, our southern skies are unguarded."

Jack twisted a lock of hair, and said aloud, "We'll need the sheet. I.think we need the sword. We can't win. There's too many. What did the Prophet say? Helen, what was the Prophet's last message?"

Helen read from her handheld.

When she was finished Jack repeated, "... floods rage, purging halls and offices of depravity then flow away."

Jack looked up, "Helen, you are not safe here. You need to get out of the building. After you spread the sheet, go out to the steps."

Jack said to Pieter, "You may go."

Pieter started to rise then sat back down.

Jack, looking down, said, "Pity, I probably saved his life chasing him here."

Helen stated, "I have no opinion on the matter."

Jack finished spraying a message of hope on the sheet.

Chapter 58 – Keys to the Abyss

Bombing from orbit should have collapsed the cave, and for the most part it did. Large smooth stone walls now lay at odd angles blocking access back to the surface of the planet, but gave enough space for climbing over and under to get to the tunnels. A crystal's vibration smoothed slippage through the time medium. Without them they were walking through clear mud. Cal especially struggled through a tight crevice, being the biggest of the lot. He looked for Petey's wide grin, but no Petey.

The left tunnel was clear of rubble, but full of footprints. The three assembled at the spot Wing Lu had chipped out the first crystals. The pocket was cut clean of any trace of the mineral.

Continuing further back even the smaller pockets were cleaned out. Past the pile of bodies and skeletons in front of the gold capped ancient, more pockets were cleared and the tunnel ended. Samaipata got them into the portal but they needed the agridot to move freely. Aleksey signaled to go.

As they passed the ancient one Cal had a memory. Climbing onto the bones and bodies he reached over to the old one's waistband and ran his fingers inside. He found nothing.

Looking back at Aleksey Cal got another idea. He looked down at the old man's feet and started moving bones aside. Inside a rib cage he spotted a small metal box. Retrieving it, he kept digging down. Reaching the stone floor he found the other metal box with Wing Lu's crystal. The Captain's had to be here. Reaching under the old one's foot bones he found it. The crystals still vibrated! Cal knew instantly when he touched them. The tunnel was brighter, his movement easier.

Cal struggled out of the pile and handed a metal box and the loose crystal to Aleksey, who was immediately affected. Cal could see his form sharpen.

Aleksey showed Nadia the plunger on his box. As they all turned back up the tunnel the traces of previous trips could now be clearly seen. Aleksey picked the one going to the backside of the cave's portal door, held Nadia's hand and disappeared. Cal hit the plunger on the metal box he retained. He bounced to the portal door. Aleksey and his sister were gone. The portal door into the cave had been shattered by the bombing. Though Cal could still see through it back into the cave, exiting the time dimension here was out of the question. No telling what damage would happen walking through the fractures, and with no more agridot accessible the temple's use was gone, except as a hub for these trails and whatever the swirling black stuff was.

Cal picked the path to Pieter's office and leaned forward. The images were more discernible now with experience traversing the torrent. A sudden flash of white caught his attention and he stepped out of the stream to find his name sprayed in big letters. One side of the white cloth was held up by an attendant, the other by an elegant lady.

She, Helen, gathered the sheet, and thanked her helper. Two security guards rushed to grab her only to trip and fall at her feet with their heads thrashing wildly until their speech was unintelligible. No assailant could be seen. A third guard stopped short with hands slightly raised. The woman walked wide eyed into the hall and turned into the hallway unaware of Cal's help.

Panicked, Cal dashed to follow only to find his progress slowed as he left the office. Cal looked back and could feel radiating vibrations from the dangling crystal light fixture with blue green points. This was the door, the other end of the portal! Each path presented from the cavern under the temple must point to another portal. The cavern must still contain massive deposits of agridot and each matching deposit or fixture a destination.

The office suddenly filled with Scythian soldiers. Cal jumped into the torrent, bouncing down to the cavern on Onyx. More soldiers there rushed at him as soon as he landed, but Cal wasn't hanging about, and shot right back up the stream, as enemies dove for his fading image.

Remaining in the stream Cal avoided Scythians and back tracked in time to find where the woman with the sheet came from. His effort finally rewarded as the woman exited an obscure door down a long passageway revealing Jack standing behind her looking ghastly but alive! Oddly, she held, of all things, a painting.

Relieved and unsure, Cal jumped backwards to the previous night. He had to find Henry.

Standing in Henry's cell Cal read the message he was to convey to Jack scratched into the wall. He knew exactly where she could find it, but how to code the getaway airport? And where was Islay Scotland? How can I find the airport code for Islay?

Chapter 59 – Blue Fire

Helen's door opened. Henry stood in the door flanked by armed security, with more filling the passage behind him.

"G'day love. See you had some dress up time."

An officer with leveled pistol said, "Come with us, Miss Jammula."

Jack raised her hands and walked out. Behind her, the painting covered the obscured remnants of Cal's message.

Walking into Pieter's office Emir Vos sat fingering the antique steel pistol, spare ammunition scattered in and out of a box.

Not looking up Vos began sliding bullets into the revolving chambers, and said, "The three people I most want dead. How nice for you to gather for me."

Henry said, "Before the killing starts you might want to locate the black sword."

Vos's eyes widened. Slowly he raised the barrel of the pistol.

Henry added, "Closest you will ever get to real magic - and power."

"Where is the sword," it wasn't a question. The statement preceded inevitable flame erupting from the revolver's gaping maw.

"Ask Jackie, here. Sword goes with her."

The pistol moved to Jack.

"Go on, tell him," Henry coaxed.

Jack nodded toward the side cabinet and a guard opened the double doors and pulled the canvas off the object, revealing the meter long black blade.

"Bring it to me," Vos commanded.

The guard's eyes widened as he struggled to lift the handle. Another guard stepped over to assist.

As the two groaned under the weight. Jack looked at Henry and nodded to the light fixture. She whispered, "Agridot."

Henry looked intently at the dangling crystal covered fixture.

Vos said, "How does this work? It's too heavy to swing."

The Prophet said, "Well don't let Jackie touch it, but I can show you."

The pistol moved back to Henry.

"These muscle men can barely move it. What's a skinny ass miner like me gonna do?"

The gun hesitated, then waved him forward.

Henry stepped forward talking to Jack, "By the way, Jackie, that's not agridot up there exactly. Agridot's a metal. Oh, the light's got bits of the stuff in the crystals. I'm guessing here, but maybe it's in a quartz matrix."

Henry's hand grabbed the sword handle and lifted it with little effort.

"How ...?"

"Yeah, sword's from a heavy gravity planet. It's been hardened and tempered with agridot. I lived on that planet for forty years, forced to lift weights sometimes sixteen hours a day. This blade's nothing."

Henry swung the blade in the air in front of Vos, and said, "Agridot turns black when fired." The air sizzled with a faint blue line and the smell of burnt ozone.

Vos' gun fired at Henry. All waited for blood and death. Nothing happened. The slugs vanished.

"Take it from him!" Vos shouted.

Henry swung in the air in front of approaching guards. Running through the blue arc the guard's torso slid apart at the angle of the arc as if the sword cut through the fabric of the room's dimension. The blue line lasted a few seconds before crackling as the dimensional break resolved. The smell remained.

Shock registered around the room, and Jack remembered Henry cutting off the warlord's head. Henry wasn't close enough, yet the head severed.

Now Henry slashed a wider gap in front of a group coming from the hallway. Jack saw through the narrow gap recognizing Scythian uniforms in a time dimension beyond. More security charged forward and hesitated at the blue line hanging in mid air. The guards in the back collided with them pushing them into the break, and their deaths. Henry turned back to Vos running for the side door. Henry flipped the sword point toward the door causing a blue line to flow out. As Vos' hand reached for the knob his hand disappeared through the cut, replaced by a savage scream.

An interrupter blast hit Henry in the back. He spun back to the hallway.

"Sonny, doesn't work on heavy gravity folk. Just pisses 'em off."

The sword flicked forward, blue energy shooting forward like water from a dish rag. Security scrambled out of the office.

"Jackie, rip that light fixture down and a bunch of the wire. Cal's gonna need it." He started slashing the air around her. The sword seemed to hesitate at times but the action continued around Jack as she stood on a chair. Pieter, cringed on the floor as events boiled around him. A rending sound followed the light's removal. Jack, standing on the ground, leaned and pulled until a snap in the ceiling released the light's cord, and three meters of wire came sliding out.

Chapter 60 – Every End's Beginning

The previous night Cal carved the message on Helen's wall and replaced the painting. He re-entered the flood. Every re-start began from Pieter's office, and he worked his way back in time to find Henry in his cell. Unaware of Cal's presence Henry slept soundly. Turning to leave Cal saw his name and a message carved in the wall.

Cal re-entered the torrent, only this time as he exited, as Henry told him to, at an electric blue flash with Scythians flying past, ignoring him. Cal jumped back. Scythian bodies, limbs, torsos littered the ground. Henry swung the black sword around Jack. The flat of the sword opened a wider gap. Henry saw what he was looking for.

"I'll have that Jackie girl," Henry said taking the fixture with wire wound around it. "You'd best find the closest exit, Darling."

He cut a large gap and forced the fixture through. It disappeared from the office and landed in front of Cal. Cal lifted it and bounced into the torrent as he had been directed.

Chapter 61 – My Head Still Hurts

Only three Scythians guarded the area behind the broken cave door. They drew knives and came at Cal. Even if he could defeat them, Cal knew time was running out somewhere. He backed away toward the pull of the central darkness, feeling it pull on his clothes and hair. The Scythians slowed their approach allowing Cal to retreat into the place they feared. Cal unwound the wire and started swinging the cluster of crystals in a widening circle. The soldiers' eyes widened and they stepped away from him. Cal looked over his shoulder to see the spinning orb drawing out vaporous filaments of darkness coming towards it.

Cal faced the soldiers again in time to see them disappear up the torrent he just came down. Looking back again, the dark mass rushed forward. Cal unbalanced cosmic forces he did not understand. The black rushed forward filling the whole dimension. Cal was aware of Aleksey and his sister arriving as he leapt forward following the Scythians, dragging the crystal fixture behind him. Events erupted out of his control.

There was no choosing his exit from the torrent, a dark boiling emptiness surged under him forcing him out into Pieter's office and through a massive gap Henry had opened. Cal landed on his feet just steps from Henry slashing the edges of the opening trying to widen it more.

Cal looked at him and Henry shouted, "Run like the devil!"

Blackness cascaded out of the opening, but instead of filling the office it pulled everything into its emptiness. including air into itself. Henry dodged guards, senators, furniture, everything flying at him to keep one hand ...

Chapter 62 – Black Flood

Cal dashed into the main hallway and through the door towards Helen's office dragging the crystal sphere banging along behind him. The roiling black flood filling the space behind him, ripping doors open on either side. Cal could feel air rushing past to join the singularity of the void coming after him.

A security door ahead opened and a startled office worker looked up at the sound of Cal's thundering footsteps. She threw papers away, dashing into the nearest door. Cal rushed by in a snow storm of papers flying past him and heard the brief trailing call for help as the door, like so many others, was ripped off the hinges. At the end of the long hallway Cal crashed through a door into a service stairway. He sprinted upward two stairs at a time. The black flood flowed down and then up giving Cal time to reach the top floor, and the long corridor across the upper offices. All along his run Cal heard behind him wreckage and screams mingled within the roar of wind.

The passageway ended with double doors into the great staircase. The black coming from behind also came from the side and through many doors on all floors having snaked its way throughout the building. The doors ahead of Cal were sucked in and disappeared. His only option remaining was down and out of the building. Blackness poured out of doors below and across. Cal grabbed the railing and jumped over.

Glimpses of soldiers with weapons, technicians, and politicians disappearing upwards, downwards, and sideways into dark, vacuous billows met him as he fell the ten floors into the pool of black coming up from below. A sudden surge jerked him sideways into the churning nothingness filling the great theater.

Somewhere in a space Pieter's office once occupied a wound in the material fabric of dimensions resolved itself. The gap slammed shut leaving Cal sliding on his butt into a demolished cavern of a room. Wires hung from the ceiling giving off sparks. Strangely, there was a clump of seats remaining. A young woman still clinging to them, weakly called for help. Cal, stiff and achy, stood and slowly made his way through the dusty air. He lifted a door wedged on top and helped her to her feet.

Chapter 63 – Now What?

Jack was about to leave Henry's side but looked back for Pieter. Pieter was gone. She raced for the back door and found him slumped against a wall staring blankly, with multiple bullet holes. Across from him, Vos was still gasping for air, bleeding out from multiple knife wounds, the antique pistol still in his hand. Not stopping, Jack bolted for the narrow hallway, and down the stairs jumping each flight. At the bottom floor she hit the crash bar bolting into the side of the main entry. She heard a crashing behind her in the stairwell. Past the bottom of the great staircase Jack ran past an army of panicked security. They did not try to stop her.

Outside, Helen waved from the temporary platform built for speakers. Jack stepped up as Helen gasped looking at the top of the building. Jack saw whispy tendrils of black forking and branching into the air from several open windows. From one window a security guard holding a rifle leapt out, hung in mid air as the black reached out to him, and pulled him back inside. A few seconds later black filled the glass covered entry way Jack just left. A loud boom shook the air and the black evaporated like a bad dream. The wind ceased. The crowd stopped and stared at the building.

Helen picked up a microphone, "Police in the crowd, open those doors. Help everyone outside. Fire brigade, give me an assessment of the damage! Move people!"

By long training, Jack's eyes turned to the crowd. She immediately spotted the man in construction dungarees staring intently at Helen. Jack pulled Helen down as the bolt flew past her. The crowd saw Jack dressed in black leap into the crowd and take the larger man down.

Helen spoke again into the mic, "There are assassins in the crowd." She stood and pointed to men running away, "Stop those men!"

Jack turned her shooter over to police and stopped, eyes wide. Cal limped out the main doors propped open, handing a scared woman over to first aid workers. Jack sprinted toward Cal. Her hug slammed into him.

Shocked and surprised, Cal paused, then wrapped his massive arms around her. Jack even found tears she thought not possible running down her cheeks.

Chapter 64 – How Do You Go Back?

Aleksey saw Cal. Then he saw the black tidal wave. The Scythian officer who discovered Aleksey and his sister over the body of Ricart Vos and charged after him into the torrent did not see the black, but, focusing on his prey, bounced to the Samaipata path. Loosing all control, Aleksey and Nadia hurled out of the stone doorway. They turned at the sound of the officer, half in, half out of the door screaming in terror. Then he was gone. The door, once again, a slab of stone.

Smelling a late afternoon wood fire and delicious smells they walked down the hill weaponless, trying unsuccessfully to create a plausible story for Scythian command. No soldiers met them, so they followed the trail of smoke into one of the open garages.

A small pig roasting over coals with parts sliced off met their excited eyes followed by a moan. Aleksey pulled back a sheet and found Petey asleep, holding the drowsy Katya.

"Petey, what you doing? Where is anyone? Where are your shoes?"

In Scythian Nadia asked the same of Katya. The empty samogon container rattled at their feet while Petey and Katya scrambled to stand and pull themselves together.

"Shoes are ... somewhere. Nobody else is about. Katya helped the last three soldiers get into the doors, and we've not seen a soul since."

Aleksey said lifting the empty container, "You drank all samogon!"

"We had to do something. You've been gone a week!"

Nadia and Katya were having a similar conversation while Petey continued, "Yeah, Katya and I were talking about starting a small farm up here. We traded with some locals for the pig and figured we'd be like Cal and Harry, start us a pig farm, but then we got hungry."

Around the evening fire, after Petey and Katya made lame excuses about being tired and left, Aleksey asked his sister, "What does she like about him?"

Nadia said, "She says he is a no farmer. She had to slaughter pig. But she says he is good mechanic, and he makes her laugh."

"But they don't speak same language."

"He is kind, and funny, and I think she loves him. Love is same language."

Chapter 65 – Finding Out

In the early morning hours large mag coils fired waking all with their deep thrum. Aleksey and Petey ran up the hill followed by the women to the only semi flat area a larger ship could land. The shiny bullet hull was tattooed with "The Nyx II."

Jamie stepped off the gangway, "Honey Badgers, we are back!"

Stories were swapped around the garage while Nadia, Katya, and Petey collected what could be salvaged. Two of the four wheelers, the samogon still, battery packs, the generator.

The tale of Angela brought tears from Jimmy Ray of all people, though all were sad.

Avinash said it best, "She went out on her own terms, and screw everyone else."

Petey said, "Denise would be proud. That was the last thing Cal told her."

"Where is Cal?" Jamie asked.

Aleksey said, "I don't know. I passed him in portal before the black pushed us out. If he is in there he did not survive."

Jamie told everyone, "We approached Samaipata looking for you when Southern Port patrols captured us. They held for three days, and just told to wait. A few hours ago they released us to come here and pick up anyone we wanted and proceed to Capital City."

Aleksey and Nadia looked at each other, but Jamie continued, "We were specifically told we would not be searched per order of the new Premier. So, no DNA scans. Anyone who wants a ride, no worries."

Aleksey asked, "What is final destination?"

Avinash said, "I'm going back to Cardea, but I can drop you off anywhere you like."

Aleksey translated. Nadia shrugged, and Katya held Petey's arm tighter.

"That settles it," Aleksey said,, "We all going."

Avinash merged the ship into the coastal thruway toward Paris at a hundred thousand meters and then onto Capital City. Radio silence was another stipulation for their search free passage.

A large delivery van pulled up to the landed transport. All cheered when the driver turned out to be Cal. The cheers faded when they saw his scowl, and they were stunned to silence when Captain Jack stepped out of the other side.

The ship's ramp lowered. Cal and Jack walked up. Shock registered on both Cal and Jack on seeing Aleksey.

Cal said, "And Nadia too! We thought you were dead! How did you make it out?"

Aleksey said, "How did you get out?" Portal on Onyx was filled. Samaipata was filled. And what was the black stuff?"

Cal said, "Henry cut an opening with the sword. The sword was made of agridot. Apparently, agridot causes these portals. The black was a portal into a gravity well of some kind, a star or black hole."

"Where is Henry," Jamie asked.

Cal sighed, "He died holding an opening for me to get out, Which reminds me," Cal said looking back into the mostly filled cargo space. "We'll need to stack the four wheelers. We have Henry's casket to load."

Jack said, "Aleksey, glad to see you. This must be Nadia. I see the family resemblance."

Petey laughed, "Yeah she looks like Aleksey but she's pretty. How does that calculate?"

Aleksey, "Hey!"

"And who is this?" Jack asked looking at the lady sitting in Petey's lap.

"This Katya." Aleksey introduced, "She is with Petey, and going to Cardea, with Nadia and me, by your permission."

"Not my permission," Jack said putting up her hands scowling. "Ask Cal. He is in charge."

"You'll need is a job and a place to live," Cal said. "Who all is going to Cardea?"

Jamie said, "I'm staying here. I've got family who needs me."

Cisco added, "I'm getting off, boss. Pancho's gone, and I want to go back to school, get gravity mill and quantum certified."

Jack counted off, "Aleksey, Nadia, Petey and Katya, Avinash has his own place. Jimmy Ray, what's your destination?"

"Cardea. You'll need a master mech."

Jack smirked, "Jimmy Ray can bunk at the hanger, and there are no more rooms at the pub. And I'm not living on a pig farm!"

Cal shot back, "I gave the farm away! I'll add on more rooms at the pub!!"

Jack leaned into Cal's personal space and cooed, "So you don't want to play house with me? No, you're living in the hanger."

Cal's mouth hung open until Katya said something in Scythian. Nadia laughed out loud, and Aleksey looked shocked but smiling.

Cal asked, "What did she say?"

Aleksey said, "Katya wants to know how many years you two have been married."

Cal and Jack looked at each other and then away.

Cal said walking off the ramp, "I need some help loading Henry's casket. It weighs a lot." To Jamie he said, "You can take the truck back to Port Security. Any food or rooms you can charge on your ID. You have the new Premier's authority."

"Who is the new Premier?" Jamie asked.

"Pieter's wife, Helen."

Cal pulled the black case to the end of the truck. "Lift with your legs, not your back." The six men lowered the casket onto the maintenance cart.

"Udivitel'no!" Aleksey said, "This little guy weighs as much as Cal! And also, you not ... em ... stutter."

Cal pushed the cart toward the ship, "I don't stutter in combat."

"Are we in combat?" Petey asked.

"I am," Cal said, "You let her make one decision and she wants to make them all!" Jack heard the comment from the top of the ramp and smiled at Cal.

Nadia shrugged and said, "Nizdevania." Katya nodded.

Cal waited for Aleksey who hesitated, but finally said, "She said 'nesting'. It means when mother birds ..."

"I know what it means!" Cal said.

Chapter 66 – Going to Cardea

Flying the Atlantic central thruway to the orbital departure point, Cal sulked in back with the cargo. Petey took a seat across the aisle repeating Jack's story of the message on the wall.

"I-L-Y, pretty bold there mate!"

"Oh, that prophet's a sneaky bugger. ILY is the airport code for Islay, Scotland! He lied to me!"

Petey's eyes widened and he said, "Oh that bastard! Tricking you into sleeping next to that hard body every night, having that beautiful face kissing you every morning - pure torture! I can't imagine the misery. I've half a mind to march right up there and set her straight."

Cal saw the smirk on Petey's face and said, "I suppose it's not all bad."

"Not bad? A gorgeous lady like that and your ugly mug - you struck gold and no question."

Cal unnecessarily whispered, "Seriously Petey, we don't talk about this, not even joke about this one."

"Cal! I'm your mate. To my grave, absolutely. And I gotta say, no woman in the galaxy would have read that message any other way. Let's go join the rest."

Past the first quantum leap Avinash asked from the copilot seat, "So you are taking over D & A Transport?"

Jack said, "I understand the businesses were left to the squad. Cal's taking over the pub. You have first choice if you want to run the hangar."

"Not me! I like flying."

Jack asked over her shoulder, "What about you, Petey? Are you and Katya ... Your room in the village is too small."

Petey looked back to the sleeping Katya and said, "I was thinking we'd take over Cooksey's place. What about you Cal?"

Cal now sitting behind the cockpit said, "I'm renaming it the Black Sword Pub. Got a replica made. It'll hang over the bar."

Petey said, "Where should we bury Henry? We could plant him next to Harry."

Cal said, "Let's keep him close, outside the pub next to Cooksey and Chico."

"How is it the sword got sucked into the black hole, but not Henry?"

Avinash noticed Jack look into the cabin mirror at Cal sitting behind her.

Cal said, "Henry was strong as old cheese. I had to pry his fingers off the pipe he clung to."

Avinash said, "I think we should make a name wall for Denise and Angela ..."

Cal said, "Wing Lu, Cooksey, Chico, ..."

Petey added, "Pancho, Kat, and Miranda ..."

After a pause Jack said, "And Harry Bolger."

Avinash, Cal, and Petey replied, "To Harry."

The End

About the Author

The author, K N Boyle, comes from an Irish American family of storytellers. Using his exposure to business, ranching, surfing, accounting, farming, engineering, religions, computers and IT, he weaves the facets of life into relatable stories of everyday people in extraordinary times.